Bridger hadn'  **here to find. N**

And now he'd ma~~de~~ Cavanaugh. She w~~as~~ slender, blue-eyed with short, curly blond hair. She didn't make him feel like such an outsider.

He'd come to town months ago, rented an old farmhouse just outside of Old Town Whitehorse and began his search, but he wasn't any closer to learning his true identity.

Unfortunately, his quest had come at a high price. The woman he believed to be the ringleader of the illegal adoptions, Pearl Cavanaugh, had suffered a stroke.

Bridger tried not to get his hopes up, telling himself that if he didn't find any adoption records, there was always Pearl's granddaughter Laci. As it turned out, she was free for Christmas.

One way or the other, maybe he'd finally get lucky.

B.J. DANIELS

THE
MYSTERY MAN
OF WHITEHORSE

HARLEQUIN®

TORONTO • NEW YORK • LONDON
AMSTERDAM • PARIS • SYDNEY • HAMBURG
STOCKHOLM • ATHENS • TOKYO • MILAN • MADRID
PRAGUE • WARSAW • BUDAPEST • AUCKLAND

This one is for good friend Al Knauber.
Hope you're loving Alaska.
We're missing you down here.

ISBN-13: 978-0-373-88798-9
ISBN-10:   0-373-88798-1

THE MYSTERY MAN OF WHITEHORSE

ABOUT THE AUTHOR

B.J. Daniels's life dream was to write books. After a career as an award-winning newspaper journalist, she sold thirty-seven short stories before she finally wrote her first book. That book, *Odd Man Out*, received a 4½ star review from *Romantic Times BOOKreviews* and was nominated for Best Harlequin Intrigue of 1995. Since then she has won numerous awards, including a career achievement award for romantic suspense.

B.J. lives in Montana with her husband, Parker, two springer spaniels, Spot and Jem, and an aging, temperamental tomcat named Jeff. When she isn't writing, she snowboards, camps, boats and plays tennis.

To contact B.J., write to her at P.O. Box 1173, Malta, MT 59538, e-mail her at bjdanielsmystery@hotmail.com or check out her Web site at www.bjdaniels.com.

Books by B.J. Daniels

HARLEQUIN INTRIGUE

*McCalls' Montana
**Montana Mystique
†Whitehorse, Montana

CAST OF CHARACTERS

Bridger Duvall—He's a mystery to the people of Whitehorse. But at least one person in town knows the truth.

Laci Cavanaugh—-She refuses to believe her best friend's death on her honeymoon was accidental.

Alyson Banning Donovan—She married the man of her dreams. Or did she?

Spencer Donovan—He didn't appear to be a killer—until you got a good look at his past.

Glen Whitaker—The reporter is determined to get to the bottom of the mystery—even if it kills him.

Emma Shane—She found falling in love to be a real killer.

Arlene Evans—She fears she's blown any chance she had of getting Mother of the Year.

Violet Evans—Anyone else would have gone crazy locked up.

Chapter One

Laci Cavanaugh blamed the champagne. Normally she didn't drink anything stronger than coffee, so of course the champagne had gone right to her head.

Her best friend's wedding called for champagne, though. Laci and Alyson Banning had been friends since birth. Like Laci, Alyson had ended up being raised by her grandparents south of Whitehorse, Montana, just down the county road from each other. And while both had left for college and careers, both were now back.

Unfortunately, Alyson's return had been bittersweet. Just weeks before her wedding, her grandfather had died. With the invitations already sent, she had stuck to her plans, knowing that's what her grandfather would have wanted. The wedding reception now had the community center jam-packed, the large room shimmering with candles and silver streamers, the air alive with laughter and happy voices.

Laci had never seen her friend so blissful, and the best news of all was that Alyson and Spencer might be staying around Whitehorse after their honeymoon. All Alyson had to do was convince Spencer, and Laci didn't think that was going to be a problem given that the man clearly idolized his new bride. Laci loved the prospect of having her best friend here. She was already fantasizing about their children growing up together.

Assuming, of course, that Laci's Prince Charming came riding up soon and swept her off her feet, as Alyson's had. It had all sounded so romantic—and, of course, being best friends, Alyson had told Laci *everything*. Love at first sight, Alyson had said. Not two weeks into the relationship she'd brought him home to meet her grandfather.

Laci had been in Billings with her cousin Maddie, so she hadn't gotten to meet Spencer that time. She'd only really got to spend any time around him at the rehearsal dinner. But she'd seen at once why Alyson had fallen for the man. He was charming and incredibly handsome, not to mention attentive and clearly crazy about Alyson.

Laci had felt a twinge of envy. Unfortunately, men like Spencer didn't come along every day. At least they hadn't for her.

As she took a sip of her champagne and watched the bride and groom dance, she was overwhelmed with happiness for her friend. The two looked so perfect together: Alyson beautiful with her long, flowing auburn hair and slender body, Spencer tall, dark and handsome as any movie star. The perfect couple.

As the dance ended, Alyson turned to say something to one of the guests. Laci found herself looking at Spencer, thinking how adorable the couple's children would be.

Spencer was smiling, his eyes on his bride as he watched her converse with the guest.

And that's when it happened.

His expression changed so quickly that Laci told herself she'd only imagined the look he gave his bride. It lasted all of a split second. Just a flicker of something dark and disturbing.

Just long enough for Laci's blood to turn to ice. Her champagne glass slipped from her fingers, shattering as loudly as a gunshot as it hit the floor. Laci didn't hear it. Nor did she see anything but the groom. It was as if only she and Spencer were in the room.

He turned his head. Maybe at the sound of the glass breaking. Or maybe he'd felt her gaze on him. His eyes locked with hers. Time stopped.

He blinked, then smiled as if he thought he could hide the fact that he was visibly shaken and upset. He *knew* she'd seen him. Laci gasped, not realizing until then that she'd been holding her breath. Music and laughter filled the space again. One of the caterer's crew rushed to clean up her broken glass and the spilled champagne.

She stumbled back, feeling weak and sick to her stomach as she watched her best friend turn back to Spencer and whisper something in his ear. They both laughed, then Spencer swept Alyson into his arms and whirled her across the dance floor.

"They make a beautiful couple, don't they?" said a tall brunette woman Laci didn't know but whose too-sweet perfume was making her sicker.

Laci could only nod, her heart beating so hard it hurt. She fought her way through the crowd to the back door, feeling suddenly faint as she told herself that she hadn't seen anything.

It was just the champagne. That and her overactive imagination. Or maybe she'd misread his look. She couldn't even be sure he'd been looking at Alyson.

Her mind raced. All she knew for sure was that the look she'd seen had been hateful and dangerous. And now her best friend was married to the man. Not just married to him, head over heels in love with him.

It made no sense. Why would Spencer marry Alyson if he didn't love her? Unless her friend was pregnant and he'd felt forced into the marriage?

But Alyson would have confided in Laci if that had been the case. Aly told her everything, didn't she?

Outside, Laci took deep, gasping breaths,

tears burning her eyes as she rushed around the side of the building to the darkness and leaned her palms against the wall of the community center and retched.

"Weddings have the same effect on me," said a deep male voice behind her.

She started, fearful that Spencer had followed her. But the voice had come from the playground of the one-room schoolhouse next door.

A man in a tuxedo rose from where he'd been sitting on the merry-go-round and walked toward her. He handed her the napkin that had been wrapped around the stem of his champagne glass. The paper cloth was cold and damp. Just what she needed.

She wiped her face, the chilly night air slowly bringing her back to her senses. "Must have been something I ate."

"Sure," he said. "Couldn't have been anything you drank." His sarcasm was at odds with the deep timbre of his voice. He was tall and solid-looking and vaguely familiar.

She took a step back and bumped into the wall.

"You really should sit down," he said.

"I need to get back inside." It was the last thing she wanted to do. Just the thought of seeing Spencer with Alyson made her feel sick again.

"Here," the man said, taking her arm. "Just sit down for a minute." He drew her over to the merry-go-round, his grip strong and sure.

"I'm fine," she protested, but she grabbed the railing and sat as her legs gave way under her.

"Yeah, you're great," he said. "If you were any better, you'd be flat on the ground."

She put her head between her knees, afraid he was right. She'd never fainted in her life, but tonight could be a first.

She told herself she'd sit for just a minute, then she had to go warn Alyson. Even as she thought it, Laci questioned the sanity of that idea. She'd spent the last twenty-nine years going off half-cocked. Never one to look before she leaped, she'd suffered the consequences of her actions, especially when it came to relationships.

Was she seriously thinking of telling

Alyson about the "look" she'd seen? Aly would never believe her, especially based on some brief, questionable glance. Laci would only come off as jealous or spiteful or both.

"You all right?" he asked as he took a seat next to her.

Out of the corner of her eye she saw him finish off his champagne and set the glass down on the ground. She mumbled, "Uh-huh."

He didn't say anything after that, just leaned back against the railing and stretched out his long legs. He wore cowboy boots with his tux. Something about that made her feel a little safer in his company.

Laci concentrated on breathing and convincing herself she was losing her mind. A better alternative than thinking that her best friend had just married not only the wrong man, but also a man who was…what? Dangerous?

After a few minutes, she sat up, feeling a little better, and glanced over at the man beside her. He was staring up at the stars, both hands behind his head, his profile serene.

"Better?" he asked, not looking at her.

"Yes. Thank you." As she heard the front door of the community center open and the crowd rush out, she pushed to her feet, still feeling a bit wobbly.

"Looks like the bride and groom are about to make their departure," her merry-go-round companion said without moving.

Laci hurried toward the excited guests. She could hear the sound of a motor. Exhaust rose into the darkness as a car was pulled around to the front of the center. Within moments Alyson and Spencer would drive away.

As Laci pushed her way through the crowd, she spotted the bride and groom. Spencer had his arm around Alyson and seemed to be searching the crowd for someone.

When he spotted Laci, he said, "There she is."

"Laci!" Alyson rushed to her and threw her arms around her. "I told Spencer I couldn't possibly leave without saying goodbye to you," she said, sounding both breathless and blissful.

"Aly," Laci said, hugging her friend tightly. "I don't want you to go."

Alyson laughed. "I'll be back in a week."

"No, listen—"

"Come on, sweetheart," Spencer said beside them. Laci felt his hand on her arm. "Let me give Laci a hug, and then we really have to get moving if we hope to make our connections tonight."

"No," Laci said, fighting the feeling that this might be the last time she saw her friend. "Aly, listen, I have to tell you—"

Spencer pulled her into a breath-stealing hug that stifled the rest of her words. Her skin crawled as he bent his head, his lips brushing her ear, and whispered, "Goodbye, Laci."

"No," she cried as she pulled back from him and tried to see her friend. "Aly!"

But Spencer had already turned and swept Alyson up as he rushed to the waiting car, the guests surging around the pair, cutting Laci off.

Laci could only watch through tears as her friend waved from the back window, the car speeding off down the road, the lights dying away in the darkness of the November night.

Chapter Two

Laci Cavanaugh woke the next morning dizzy, headachy and sick to her stomach.

"How much did you drink last night?" she asked her image in the bathroom mirror and groaned. It was so unlike her to overindulge. She didn't even sample the wine when she was cooking, although most chefs did.

After the bride and groom had taken off, the bridesmaids had insisted Laci go into town with them to one of the bars. She'd been in a daze. She vaguely remembered the bartender having to ask them to leave at closing time. No wonder she felt so horrible.

But as she stared into the mirror she knew it wasn't just the drinks that had made her sick this morning. It was that niggling worry that she had tried to kill last night with alcohol. Alyson. Her best friend was in trouble.

Or was she?

This morning, in the light of day, Laci had to question everything that had happened last night at the reception. What had she *really* seen? A split second of something dark and disturbing on Spencer Donovan's face. She couldn't even be sure it had been directed at Alyson.

True, Laci had thought a second later that when he'd looked at her he'd been upset—as if he'd realized she'd seen him. She remembered how rattled she'd felt, how convinced he meant Alyson harm.

This morning, though, she admitted it was probably the champagne. Or her imagination—which, as her older sister Laney often pointed out, was more often than not out of control.

Even the way Spencer had said goodbye to Laci could have been innocent enough. Only *she* could read something into "Goodbye, Laci." Just as she could have imagined that he'd rushed Alyson off in such a hurry because he was afraid of what Laci would say.

She sighed. As if there had been anything she could have said to Alyson to keep her from going. She cringed at the thought of what she *might* have said. *I saw your new husband look at you funny. Like he hated you. I think he wants you dead.* Great thing to tell someone right before they take off on their honeymoon.

Wandering into the kitchen, she poured herself a large glass of orange juice. To make matters worse, she recalled her behaviour in front of the man in the school playground. He'd looked so familiar, but she couldn't place him now any more than she could last night. Not that it mattered.

Taking a sip of orange juice, she eyed the phone. Even if she could have called Alyson—who would now be on a flight to Hawaii for her honeymoon—she wouldn't have, she assured herself.

Besides, what would she say to her friend? By all appearances, Spencer seemed to be the perfect husband. Attentive, handsome, obviously educated, successful and well-off financially. Plus, Alyson adored him.

"You're wrong about him," Laci said with false conviction as she picked up the phone and dialed her sister's cell. Laney was the sensible one. That's why Laci always used her as a sounding board. And right now she needed sensible—even if her sister was on her own honeymoon.

BRIDGER DUVALL STOOD in the middle of the musty building in downtown Whitehorse, telling himself he should have gone with his first instinct and left town.

"What do you think?" the young Realtor asked. She was a cute blonde with a husband and at least one young son and was so green that he suspected this could be her first sale.

What did he *think*? He thought he should have his head examined. He looked around the building. The structure had been sitting empty for a couple of years at least. Which should have told him that opening *any* business in this town was more than a little risky, but a restaurant was crazy.

The building needed to be completely remodeled. Fortunately, he could do a lot of the work himself.

As he stood there, he could imagine the brick walls with art on them, cloth-covered tables along both sides with candles glowing, low music playing in the background and some alluring scents coming out of the kitchen at the back.

If he closed his eyes, he could almost smell his marinara sauce and hear the clatter of dishes, the murmur of voices and, of course, the comforting ding of the cash register.

"It would need a lot of work," the Realtor said.

An understatement. "It would need a *whole* lot of work." But even as he said it he knew he was going to take the place. There was plenty of light, the building was more than adequate for what he wanted to do and the price was right. With luck, he could be open before Christmas.

It wouldn't be the restaurant of his dreams. Not in this isolated part of the state. But since he couldn't leave here, he might as well do something while he was waiting.

"Let's write up an offer," he said and saw the Realtor's surprise.

"Really?"

He laughed. "You talked me out of every other place in town."

"Maybe I should try to talk you out of this one."

"Don't waste your breath." He looked around him, seeing again the dust and dirt and peeling paint. Still… "There is something about this place."

She followed his gaze, clearly not seeing it. "Well, if you're sure this is the building you want…"

He smiled at her. "It is." Wait until the residents of Old Town Whitehorse heard he was opening a restaurant. It would be a clear message to them: he was staying until he got what he wanted. Or until he went broke, he thought with a wry smile.

"DO YOU HAVE ANY IDEA what time it is out here?" Laney Cavanaugh Giovanni asked, sounding half-asleep as she answered the phone.

Laci hadn't thought about the time difference between Whitehorse, Montana, and Honolulu. "Sorry. I needed someone to talk to."

"You should get a pet. Or just talk to yourself."

"I *am* talking to myself. I just don't like the answers I'm getting." Laci could hear her sister get up, then the sound of glass doors opening and closing as Laney took the phone outside. She could imagine the view of the ocean, the smell of salty sea air, the lull of the surf below the balcony and the cries of the gulls. Every woman she knew was on her honeymoon.

"How was Alyson's wedding?" Laney asked after a big yawn. But she sounded more awake. And it wasn't as though Laci would have let her go back to sleep—and she would know that.

"It was…nice."

"*Nice?*" Laney asked. "Okay, what happened? You didn't do anything you shouldn't have, did you?"

Now that she had her sister on the phone, Laci wasn't sure she wanted to tell her. It sounded too nuts, even for her. "Of course not. Look, it's nothing. Really. Sorry I woke you up. I should let you go."

"Oh, no, you don't. What is it?" her sister demanded.

Laci groaned. "You're going to think I've lost my mind."

"I already think you're nuttier than peanut brittle," Laney said, repeating something their grandmother Pearl always used to say before a stroke had left her incapacitated in a nursing home.

"Okay, something *did* happen. At least I think it did. It was probably just my imagination. I'm sure it was."

"*Laci!*"

"It's Alyson's husband, Spencer."

"Do not tell me he made a pass at you at the reception."

"No," Laci said. It was much worse than that. "I caught him looking at Alyson strangely."

"How strangely?" Laney asked, sounding as if she was taking this seriously.

Laci realized she'd hoped that her sister would tell her what a fool she was and relieve her mind. "He looked as if he couldn't stand the sight of her. As if he hated her. As if he wanted to harm her." The words were out and she wished she could call them back. She felt as if she was being disloyal to her best friend. "I know it sounds round the bend—"

"How was he acting right before that?"

"That's just it. He was laughing and smiling and dancing with her as if he couldn't believe how lucky he was to have married her. I'm sure I must be mistaken."

She groaned, remembering the look Spencer had given her when he'd felt her watching him. He'd been upset, hadn't he?

"That is really odd," Laney said. "You're sure he was looking at Alyson?"

"No. But since he doesn't know anyone else in town, who else *could* he have been looking at? Like I said, it was just for an instant. I'm probably wrong."

She waited for her sister to agree, but instead Laney asked, "Have you seen Alyson since?"

"No. Right after that they left on their honeymoon." She recalled the way Spencer had hustled Aly off. "Just tell me that I'm silly to be worried about her."

Her sister seemed to hesitate. "You're silly to worry about her."

The words lacked conviction but Laci felt better. "Speaking of honeymoons…"

"Yes, I probably should get back to mine," Laney said, a smile in her voice.

"You know that I will always suspect that you eloped so you wouldn't have to ask me to cater your reception," Laci said.

Laney laughed. "I eloped because I've decided to become more impulsive, like you."

"I don't think that's a good idea," Laci said in all seriousness. "One of us has to be the stable one. I like it when it's you."

"Eloping was the first impulsive thing I've ever done. You're the one who always told me to go with my feelings instead of being so analytical."

"I don't know why you would take advice from me."

"Maybe we'll have a reception when we get back," Laney said. "And you can cater it."

"Okay," Laci said but without her usual enthusiasm. Her mind was back on Alyson.

"We can talk more when I get home. It won't be that long, which is why I'm resuming my honeymoon *now*," Laney said, and Laci could tell by her sister's tone that Nick had joined her on the balcony. Nick was gorgeous and crazy in love with her big sister. "'Bye, sis."

"Oh, Laney, I forgot to tell you. Alyson and Spencer are spending their honeymoon in Hawaii, too. Maybe you'll run into them." But Laci realized her sister had already hung up.

AFTER WRITING UP AN offer for the building, Bridger Duvall spent the rest of the day digging through old newspaper archives, looking for any mention of Dr. Holloway, the Whitehorse Sewing Circle or Pearl Cavanaugh.

As he searched, he thought of Pearl's granddaughter Laci and their chance meeting at the wedding. Fate? Not likely given the size of Whitehorse, Montana. Laci lived five miles south of town in what was locally known as Old Town. The now near ghost town had once been Whitehorse. That was, until the railroad came through in the 1800s and the town moved north to the rails, taking the name with it.

He recalled the first time he'd seen Old Town. If a tumbleweed hadn't rolled across the dirt street in front of his car, he wouldn't have slowed and would have missed the place entirely.

Little was left of the small ranching community. At one time there'd been a gas station, but that building was sitting empty, the pumps long gone. There was a community center, which was still called Whitehorse Community Center. Every small community in this part of Montana had one of those. And there was the one-room schoolhouse next to it.

There were a few houses, one large one that was boarded up, a Condemned sign nailed to the door, an old shutter banging in the wind.

For years the community had been run by Titus and Pearl Cavanaugh, both descendents of early homesteaders and just as strong and determined as the first settlers.

Titus was as close to a mayor as Old

Town had. He provided a church service every Sunday morning at the community center and saw to the hiring of a school-teacher when needed.

Pearl's mother Abigail had started the Whitehorse Sewing Circle. The women of the community got together a few times a week to make quilts for every new baby and every newlywed in the area.

The old cemetery on the hill had also kept the Whitehorse name. The iron on the sign that hung over the arched entrance was rusted but readable: Whitehorse Cemetery.

Bridger had learned a lot about the area just stopping at a café in Whitehorse proper, five miles to the north and the last real town for miles. All he'd had to do was ask about Old Town Whitehorse and he got an earful. The people were clannish and stuck to them-selves. The old-timers still resented the town moving and taking the name. And, like Whitehorse proper, both communities were dying.

A lack of jobs was sending the younger residents to more prosperous parts of the state or the country. The population in the entire county was dropping each year. People joked about who would be around to turn the lights out when Whitehorse completely died.

While Bridger had learned a lot, he hadn't gotten what he'd come here to find. Not yet, anyway.

And now he'd made the acquaintance of Pearl's granddaughter, Laci. She was a cute thing, fair skinned, slender, with short curly blond hair and blue eyes.

Life was strange, he thought as he continued to search the old newspapers. In a way, his life had started here. And now here he was, thirty-two years old and back here in hopes of finding himself.

The one thing he'd learned quickly was that being an outsider was a disadvantage in a small Montana town. Not that he'd expected to be accepted immediately just because he lived here and was now opening a restaurant.

But he'd found it was going to take time. Fortunately, time was the one thing he had plenty of.

His eye caught on a notice in one of the old

newspapers he'd been thumbing through. A city permit for a fence at a house owned by the late Dr. Holloway.

Bridger felt a rush of excitement. For months he'd been trying to track down his birth mother after finding out that he was adopted.

Not just adopted—illegally adopted. The story his adoptive mother told him on her deathbed involved a group of women called the Whitehorse Sewing Circle.

Thirty-two years ago, his parents, both too old to adopt through the usual channels, had gotten a call in the middle of the night telling them to come to the Whitehorse Cemetery.

There an elderly woman gave them a baby and a birth certificate. No money exchanged hands. Nor names. Bridger had surmised over his time here that the woman in the cemetery that night was none other than Pearl Cavanaugh.

How a group of women had decided to get into the illegal adoption business was still beyond him. Nor did he know how many babies had been placed over the years.

He'd come to town months ago, rented an old farmhouse just outside of Old Town and begun his search.

Unfortunately, his quest had come at a high price. Most of the people involved were now dead. The doctor who Bridger believed had handled the adoptions—Dr. Holloway—had been murdered by one of his coconspirators, his office building burned to the ground, all records apparently lost.

The woman he believed to be the ringleader, Pearl Cavanaugh, had suffered a stroke. Another key player, an elderly women named Nina Mae Cross, had Alzheimer's. Both women were in the nursing home now. Neither was able to tell him anything.

But Bridger was convinced Holloway was too smart to keep records of his illegal adoption activities with his patients' medical records at the office. So he held out hope that the records would be found elsewhere.

But where would the doctor have hidden them to make sure they never surfaced? Maybe in this house Bridger had discovered.

Or maybe no records had been kept. Certainly no charges had been filed against anyone involved, for lack of evidence.

But even if Bridger found proof, not one of the women in the original Whitehorse Sewing Circle was less than seventy now. None would ever see prison. The only thing he could hope for was learning his true identity.

"Even if you had proof that would stand up in court," the sheriff had said, "you sure you want these women thrown in jail? If they hadn't gotten you and your twin sister good homes, neither of you might be alive today."

Bridger knew he probably owed his life to the Whitehorse Sewing Circle. The women had taken babies who needed homes and placed them with loving couples who either couldn't conceive or were ineligible to adopt because of their age.

Also, something good had come out of his quest: he'd found his twin sister, Eve Bailey. Eve had grown up in Old Town and suspected from an early age that she was adopted. She'd come back here also looking for answers and, like him, had ended up staying.

As he copied down the address of the house that Dr. Holloway had owned, he felt a surge of hope. The doctor had lived in an apartment over his office. So what had he used the house for?

Bridger tried not to get his hopes up, telling himself that if he didn't find anything at the house, there was always Pearl Cavanaugh's granddaughter.

One way or the other, maybe he'd finally get lucky.

LACI JUMPED WHEN THE phone rang and picked it up before even checking caller ID. She'd been thinking about Alyson, so she'd just assumed it would be her.

"Laci?"

"Maddie?" She realized she hadn't heard from her cousin in weeks, not since Maddie Cavanaugh had moved to Bozeman to attend Montana State University. "How are you?"

"Great. Really great," Maddie said, sounding like her old self again.

Laci couldn't have been more relieved.

Maddie had been through so much, not the least being suspected of murder. But probably the hardest was her breakup with her fiancé, Bo Evans.

The hold Bo had on Maddie was still a concern. Laci feared that Maddie might weaken and go back to that destructive relationship.

"So tell me about your classes," Laci said, and Maddie launched into an enthusiastic rundown. She sounded so happy that Laci began to relax a little.

Counseling and college seemed to have helped Maddie put Bo Evans and a need to punish herself behind her.

Maddie asked about Laci's catering business, and Laci quickly changed the subject. Her lack of business was the least of her worries right now, but she didn't want to get into the Alyson and Spencer situation with her cousin.

"I have a test first thing in the morning, so I'd better go," Maddie said after they'd talked for a while. "I wanted to let you know that my roommate has invited me home for Christmas. She's from Kalispell, so…"

Laci tried to hide her disappointment. Maddie had planned to spend Christmas with her. Laney and Nick had already made plans to have Christmas with his family in California. "Oh, you'll have a great time. What a nice invitation."

"You don't mind?" Maddie asked, sounding relieved.

"Of course I will miss you, but I'm so glad you're enjoying college and making friends." Laci knew that Laney would now insist she come to California—the last thing she wanted to do. Christmas required snow. Christmas was Montana. Also, she couldn't leave her grandfather alone for the holidays.

"I'm really proud of you," Laci said. "You've been through a lot."

"You know us Cavanaugh women," Maddie said with a laugh. "I'm excited about the future." Her cousin sounded surprised by that. After everything she'd been through, it was no wonder.

Laci hung up, relieved that Maddie hadn't asked about Bo Evans. Maybe she was finally over him. Laci would rather believe that than believe Maddie hadn't wanted to come home for Christmas because she was afraid to see Bo again. Either because she feared she might be tempted or because she was scared of the Evans family. Laci could understand being afraid of *that* family.

ARLENE EVANS COULDN'T believe the mental hospital wouldn't let her see her daughter Violet.

"I told you they wouldn't let us in," Charlotte said as she inspected the ends of her long blond hair.

Arlene glanced over at her younger daughter as she put the car into gear. More and more, Charlotte was starting to annoy her. The whiny voice. The obsession with her split ends. The way she'd put on weight since the "incidents."

Arlene insisted the family all refer to the attempts on her life as "those unfortunate *incidents*" if they had to refer to them at all. She would just as soon forget the whole thing. But that was a little difficult since the entire country had heard about her three children trying to kill her.

It had almost cost Arlene the farm in

lawyer fees to get her two youngest off. It *had* cost her her husband. Floyd divorced her and ran off with some grain seed saleswoman. Good riddance. She'd leased out the land and would be just fine now that her Rural Meet-A-Mate Internet dating service was doing so well. Being on national TV hadn't hurt.

Whatever the cost, it had been worth it to get Charlotte and Bo cleared. In her own mind, Arlene knew where the blame for the whole mess lay: her old-maid daughter Violet. Violet had always been the problem child. Charlotte, barely eighteen, and Bo, now twenty, would never have even contemplated the terrible things they'd done without Violet as the ringleader.

Alice Miller, that old busybody who lived down the road, had suggested the children were fed too much sugar. The woman really needed to turn off the talk-show television and take care of her own business.

Fortunately, Arlene had been able to hire a good lawyer for Charlotte and Bo and got them probation. The judge had insisted they come home and live with her so they could begin to heal. Arlene wasn't sure that's what had been going on at the house, though.

Bo stayed in his room listening to that horrible music and barely had a civil word for her, except late at night when he went out doing who knew what. Charlotte, restricted from going into town on Saturday nights because of those other unfortunate *incidents* involving strange men, hung around the house and ate.

Half the time, Arlene couldn't stand the sight of her own children. Now *there* was an episode for the talk shows.

The only way she'd been able to stay sane was to concentrate on her business. Her Internet rural dating business had taken off after she'd been interviewed on one of the national morning TV shows. But many locals were still wary of the Internet. She'd been forced to remove some people's profiles who hadn't asked to be put on her Web page. The ingratitude of people still amazed her.

Like the Cavanaughs. The whole bunch of them blamed Bo for Maddie's problems. All Arlene could say was good riddance to that one, too. She hated to think what Bo's life would have been like if he'd married that girl.

Arlene couldn't believe the injustice in the world. That's probably why, when she got to the point that she found herself finding fault with Charlotte and Bo, she would turn all her anger and frustration on the one person who really deserved it—her oldest daughter, Violet. On the fast track to thirty-five and insane, Violet had little chance of ever getting married now. And wasn't it just like everyone to blame the mother for it.

"I'd love to give Violet a piece of my mind," Arlene said as she left the mental hospital, tires spitting gravel. She'd even hired a lawyer, but the hospital hadn't budged, saying that it would not be in Violet's best interest to see her mother. As if Arlene gave a fig about Violet's best interest.

Did Violet appreciate all the years Arlene had labored tirelessly to try to get her married off? No. How did Violet pay her back? She'd tried to kill her own mother and had drawn in her younger sister and brother as accomplices.

"Sometimes I just don't know why I try," Arlene said and sighed as she drove toward Old Town Whitehorse. Beside her, Charlotte pulled a candy bar from her jacket pocket, at least her third this morning.

"Watch where you're going!" Charlotte yelled as the car almost went off the road. "What is your *problem?*"

Arlene got the car back on the road and looked over at her daughter again. She'd never noticed before how much Charlotte was beginning to resemble her sister Violet.

BACK AT THE HOSPITAL, Violet Evans felt the drool run down her chin but didn't move a muscle to stop it.

"Violet?"

She stared into nothingness, her eyes glazed over, her mind miles away. Miles away in Old Town Whitehorse.

"Violet, can you hear me?"

The doctors called her condition a "semi-catatonic state." She'd been like this ever since she'd been brought to the mental hospital after admitting to trying to kill her mother. It was a textbook-classic case, she'd heard the doctors say and had to suppress the urge to laugh.

It *should* be textbook-classic; that's where she'd found the symptoms for the condition. Lately, though, the doctors had noticed that she was starting to come out of it.

Violet loved fooling with them. One day soon she would come out of it, all right. She wouldn't remember anything. When they told her about her crimes, she would be shocked, feel incredible remorse for the misery she'd caused and find it almost unbearable.

There would be suspicion with her apparent confusion about where she'd been, what she'd done. There would be more psychiatric tests, but finally they would have to release her back into society. They would have to since she'd clearly been sick when she'd tried to kill her own mother. And soon she would be well.

But for now, Violet Evans saw nothing, felt nothing, was nothing. At least on the surface. Her mind worked 24-7, planning and plotting for the day when she would walk out the front door of the hospital a free woman.

Inside, she smiled to herself. It wouldn't be long now. Soon she would be free. Only this time she would be much smarter. This time she wouldn't get caught. Nor was she just going to finish the job she'd started. That was the problem with too much time to think—it made you realize there were a lot of people you wouldn't mind seeing dead.

THE PHONE RANG THE minute Laci hung up from talking with her cousin. She smiled as she picked up the receiver, sure it was Maddie calling her back.

"What did you forget to tell me?" she said without bothering to say hello.

Silence.

"Maddie?"

No answer.

She checked the caller ID. Blocked. Her heart began to pound as she recognized the faint sound of someone breathing on the other end of the line.

She told herself there was nothing to be frightened about. It was just a bad connection. Then why could she hear the breathing just fine? "Hello?"

Still no answer.

"What do you want?" she demanded into the phone.

The caller hung up with a click.

Her heart drummed in her chest as she tried to convince herself it was just a wrong number. She hung up and hit star-6-9.

The recording confirmed that the phone number could not be accessed.

She hung up, telling herself she was over-reacting. As usual. But now she was spooked, the call feeling like an omen.

Chapter Three

At the sound of a car, Laci wandered into the living room, still feeling under the weather. And while she was relieved about Maddie, she couldn't get Alyson out of her mind. Or the strange phone call.

One of Alyson's bridesmaids, a younger friend they'd both grown up with, trotted up the front steps.

Laci opened the door, glad to see McKenna Bailey. McKenna, all cowgirl, was dressed in jeans, western shirt, boots and a straw western hat pulled down over her blond hair.

"I guess I don't need to ask how *you're* feeling," McKenna said with a laugh. "I couldn't believe you last night. I've never seen you drink that much."

Which could partly explain why she felt so horrible. But she knew the perfect cure of whatever ailed her.

"Pancakes," Laci said drawing McKenna into the kitchen.

"*Pancakes?* You can't be serious," McKenna said as she took off her cowboy hat and set it on the stool next to her at the breakfast bar.

"Pumpkin pancakes." As Laci whipped up the batter, she began to feel better. Cooking always did that for her. McKenna talked about the wedding ceremony, the food at the reception—the town women had insisted on doing a potluck, almost as if there were a plot against Laci and her catering company.

Ever since she'd decided to start Cavanaugh Catering, nothing had gone right. True, her first catered party had ended with a woman being poisoned to death—not Laci's fault, though.

Since then, she hadn't had any business and was starting to wonder if her sister had been right about it being a mistake to run a catering business here in the middle of nowhere.

Laci spooned some of the golden batter into a sizzling-hot skillet. The smell alone made her feel better.

"Spencer is really something, huh?" McKenna said.

Laci shot a look over her shoulder at McKenna. "He's handsome enough," she said noncommittally.

McKenna laughed. "Arlene Evans is positive she's seen him in one of her movie magazines." She lowered her voice. "But you should have heard what Harvey Alderson said."

Laci could well imagine, knowing Harvey.

"He said the guy looked like a porn star to him," McKenna said and laughed again. "Makes you wonder what Harvey knows about porn stars, doesn't it?"

Laci laughed and turned back to her cooking. The pancakes had bubbled up nicely. She flipped each one, then brought out the apple-cinnamon syrup and fresh creamery butter and put them on the counter in front of McKenna, happy her friend had stopped by. She wished McKenna was home for more than the weekend.

"The thing about men as good-looking as Spencer Donovan—you'd have to keep him corralled at home," McKenna said, only half joking. "Every woman in the county would be after him. Speaking of men...I did something really stupid last night."

Laci couldn't imagine McKenna Bailey doing anything stupid in her life. She hadn't even had that much to drink last night. "What?"

"I signed up on Arlene Evans's rural dating Internet site," McKenna said and grimaced. "I'm never going to find my handsome cowboy helping Eve with the ranch. Or at vet school. I figured, what would it hurt, you know?"

"I know," Laci said with a laugh as she slid a plateful of silver-dollar pancakes in front of McKenna and watched her slather them with butter before making another skilletful for herself.

Was that all it had been last night? A splash of champagne and a shot of envy, stirred not shaken, with a healthy dose of vivid imagination? She sure hoped so because she really didn't want her friend to be in trouble. She glanced at the kitchen clock over the stove as she sat down, not even hungry for her favorite pancakes. Alyson would be in Honolulu soon.

"Laci, these pancakes are to die for," McKenna said between bites. And the conversation turned to Laci's catering business—and lack of clients. And for a while Laci stopped worrying about Alyson and worried instead about how to get Cavanaugh Catering cooking.

BRIDGER DUVALL SNAPPED on his flashlight as he descended the rickety basement stairs of Dr. Holloway's former house. It was dusty and dark down here, the overhead light dim. The place, he'd learned, had been sitting empty for years. He doubted anyone had been down here in all that time.

"Can't be much of interest down there, but you're welcome to look, I guess," the elderly neighbor said from the top of the stairs.

"Thanks," Bridger called over his shoulder as he descended deeper. He'd managed to talk the neighbor into letting him into the house after discovering it was empty, and the man thought he knew where there might be a key.

In a town like Whitehorse, neighbors were often given a spare key to the house next door. Bridger loved that about this part of Montana. As it turned out, the door hadn't even been locked.

A house that the doc owned—but apparently had never lived in—seemed like the perfect place to store records you didn't want anyone to ever see.

The basement smelled of dampness and mildew. He stopped on the bottom stair. He heard something scurry across one dark corner and shot his flashlight beam in that direction quick enough to catch the shape of a mouse before it disappeared into a hole in the concrete.

Great. Who knew what else lived down here.

Bridger shone the flashlight around the small, damp basement. It was little more than a root cellar. He brushed aside the cobwebs to peer into a hole that ran back under the house. There was a lot of junk down here, most of it looking as if it had been there since the house was originally built a hundred years before.

One box held what appeared to be women's clothing. He held up one of the dresses. Dated. Had the clothes belonged to the doctor's wife before her death? Or had the doctor had a mistress who'd lived here?

Bridger dug through several of the boxes, finding more old clothing but no files. No records.

He couldn't help his disappointment. He'd hit one dead end after another. In the last box he opened he found an old photo album. He flipped it open. Most of the pages were empty except for a few colored photographs of two little girls. Children who'd been part of the adoption ring?

Tucking the album under his jacket, Bridger climbed up out of the basement, anxious for some fresh air.

The helpful neighbor was waiting in the living room. "Find anything?" he asked.

"Nothing much." He'd told the old man that he was looking for his mother's medical records. No lie there. He feared the man wouldn't let him take the photo album if he told him about it, so he kept it hidden under his jacket.

Bridger handed him back the key, thanked him and took one last look at the inside of the house, wondering why Dr. Holloway had kept it and whose clothing that was downstairs. The dresses had been in different sizes, so that seemed to rule out a mistress.

A thought struck him, giving him a chill. Was it possible the birth mothers had stayed here in this house until they'd given birth? Maybe even Bridger's own mother?

The used furniture appeared to be a good thirty years old and was now covered in dust. If his mother had stayed here, there was no sign of her after all this time.

He followed the old man out the front door, glancing back only once. For just a split second he imagined a woman standing at the front window, her belly swollen with the fraternal twins she carried, her face lost behind the dirty window.

To keep from calling Alyson and ruining her honeymoon, Laci tried to stay busy. She cooked everything she could think to make, then had to find a home for all the food.

She dropped off a week's meals at her grandfather Titus's apartment—the one he'd taken in town so he could spend more time at his wife's bedside at the nursing home.

Gramma Pearl's condition hadn't changed since her stroke. Her eyes were open, but she wasn't able to respond, even though Laci liked to believe she knew her and understood what Laci said to her. Once, Laci would have sworn her grandmother squeezed her hand. Laney said it must have been her imagination.

Laci's imagination was legendary.

The treats Laci had baked she took to the staff at the rest home when she went to visit her grandmother. They all seemed to love her cookies and cakes.

As she came out of the nursing home, Laci was debating what to do with the batch of her famous spicy meatballs she had in her car. They were too spicy for— She collided with what felt like a brick wall, emitting an "ufft" as strong arms grabbed her to keep her from toppling over backward.

"We really have to quit meeting like this," said a teasing male voice.

She looked up as she recognized the voice from the wedding reception. Actually, from the merry-go-round in the schoolyard next to the community center, where he'd come to her assistance.

"Oh, it's you," she said, embarrassed.

"Nice to see you, too," he said and grinned. "Glad to see you've recovered from the wedding. Still having trouble staying on your feet, though, I see."

He was even better looking in broad daylight. He wore a western shirt, jeans and boots. His dark hair curled at the nape of his neck beneath his gray Stetson. She noted that his clothing was worn and dusty as if he'd been working.

She hadn't taken him for a working cowboy last night—even though he'd been wearing boots with his tux. Apparently he was the real thing. Having grown up in old Whitehorse, she had a soft spot for cowboys. Especially ones as gallant as this one.

"Still rescuing damsels in distress, I see,"

she said, cringing inside at the memory of what happened at the wedding.

He smiled and held out his hand. "I don't think we were ever officially introduced. Bridger Duvall."

Bridger Duvall? The mystery man of Old Town Whitehorse? Now she remembered why he'd seemed vaguely familiar. While their paths had never crossed, she'd certainly heard about him.

"Laci Cavanaugh," she said, taking his hand. It was wonderfully large and warm and comforting. There was something so chivalrous about him. She recalled how he'd given her his napkin outside the community center. Also how he'd given her peace and quiet. She'd appreciated both.

"Nice to meet you," he said, looking into her eyes before letting go of her hand.

"So you're Bridger Duvall," she said, feeling more than a little off-kilter considering the way their paths had crossed both times.

"The scurrilous rumors about me are highly exaggerated," he said with a twinkle in his dark eyes.

She cocked her head at him, curious and maybe flirting just a little. He did have a great handshake, and that voice of his was so wonderfully deep and soft. Like being bathed in silk.

"Which rumors are those?" she asked.

"That I only come out at night, that I'm fabulously wealthy and that I'm doing weird experiments in the barn out on the ranch."

She liked his sense of humor. "And how are they exaggerated?"

Grinning, he leaned toward her conspiratorially. "I do the weird experiments in the basement."

"That house doesn't have a *basement*."

Bridger laughed as they walked toward their vehicles. "Caught me."

Laci Cavanaugh. Granddaughter of Pearl Cavanaugh. He felt only a twinge of guilt. It had been no accident running into her today. He hadn't meant the run-in to be so literal, though. But whatever worked.

"Well, at least now I know which rumors *are* true," she said as she moved to her car and started to open the door.

"It was nice seeing you again," he said,

surprised he meant it—and not because of his ulterior motive.

She smiled. "I'm sure we'll run into each other again."

As she opened her car door, he was hit with a tantalizing aroma that took his breath away. "What is that wonderful scent?" he asked stepping over to lean past her into the open car door to take a whiff.

She laughed. "Meatballs and spaghetti. I was planning to drop the dish off at the senior center, but I'm afraid it's too spicy for their tastes."

Bridger cocked a brow at her. "Well, it *is* almost dinnertime, and I just happen to know the perfect place to take it. I can assure you it would be greatly appreciated. Just follow me. It's only a few blocks from here."

He saw her hesitate, as if worried that the rumors about him might be true, before accepting. If she only knew.

Laci followed his pickup, surprised when he turned into a spot in front of one of the old empty buildings on the main street, and wondered if she hadn't made a mistake in coming here with him.

"I don't understand," she said, looking from him to the building, which apparently was being remodeled.

"You will." He opened her car door and took out the casserole dish. "Right this way."

He led her through the front of the restaurant, which was filled with sawhorses, tools, dust and paint supplies, through two swinging doors that led to the new stainless-steel commercial kitchen. Everything but a small table and two chairs was covered with plastic until the painting was finished.

Clearly this was where he'd been working. He put the casserole on the round table and dug under the plastic to open a cabinet and bring out dishes.

"I have some leftover bread and a salad I'd planned to eat for supper," he said, setting both on the table.

"What is this place?" she asked, looking back toward the front of the building as he began to cut thick slices of the bread.

"It's a restaurant. Well, that is, it will be once it's finished," he said with obvious pride, and she realized he worked here.

"Opening a new restaurant in Whitehorse?" She hadn't meant to sound so disbelieving.

"I know it's risky—"

"*Risky* is one way of putting it." She wondered who'd take such a risk, since the last restaurant in this building hadn't lasted six months.

She lifted the lid on the casserole, and he groaned and breathed in the rich scent with obvious pleasure. She couldn't help but smile with pleasure of her own.

"If that tastes half as good as it smells…"

She laughed as she dished him up some of the meatballs and spaghetti hiding beneath the sauce and waited as he sat down and picked up his fork.

He took a bite, closing his eyes and savoring the wonderful flavors. His eyes flew open. "Who made this?"

"I bought it from some woman cooking beside the road," she joked, thinking he must be doing the same, as she filled her plate and took a bite of his salad. "This salad is wonderful. Did the restaurant's cook make it?"

He grinned. "Yeah, you like?"

She nodded, looking surprised as she took a bite of the bread. "Yum. Homemade bread. Maybe this restaurant will do all right after all."

"Maybe, if it has these meatballs on the menu," he said and took another bite. "I'm serious," he said between bites. "I'm hiring whoever made this."

"Hiring them to do what?" Laci asked.

"*Cook*, what else?"

She glanced toward all the stainless steel in the kitchen. "This is *your* restaurant?"

It hadn't dawned on her. For some reason, she'd just assumed he was doing the construction on the place—not that he owned it—given how he was dressed.

About then she noticed that he was looking at her oddly. "*You* made this?" he asked, sounding as surprised as she'd been about him.

She bristled. "Don't I look like someone who could have made this?" She realized her skin was a little thin since her catering business had gone nowhere fast.

He still looked stunned, and she realized he had to be regretting saying he wanted to hire whoever had made the meatballs now that he'd found out it was her. "Is this about the job offer? Because if it is, I'm definitely not looking for a job."

"Sorry, it's just that…" He shook his head. "Can you cook anything else?"

She bristled again. "Of course. I can cook *anything*."

"That's big talk," he said, his tone challenging. "I assume you're willing to back it up?"

She glared across the table at him. "Name your terms."

He grinned. "I can have the kitchen ready tomorrow. Say 9:00 a.m.? You don't mind a little friendly competition?"

"You mean from your chef?"

He nodded, looking pleased with himself.

Not that she had to prove anything with her cooking. But damn if she wasn't going to show him. She smiled across the table at him, wanting to cook something that would knock this cowboy and his chef on their ears.

They ate in a strangely companionable silence. She couldn't remember a meal she'd enjoyed as much. After they'd finished, she started to pick up her casserole dish, but he put a hand over hers. There were only two meatballs and just a little sauce and spaghetti left.

"Mind if I finish that off later? I'd be happy to get your dish back to you tomorrow."

She looked into his dark eyes, surprised that she hadn't noticed before the tiny flecks of gold in all that warm-brownie chocolate. What was she thinking taking a cooking dare from this man?

She didn't want a job in a restaurant. She was determined to make Cavanaugh Catering a success.

But she couldn't let him think that she was a one-dish cook. No way. Her pride was at stake here.

And not just that, Laci realized as she left and headed home. Bridger Duvall had taken her mind off worrying about Alyson for a while. And for that she was thankful.

But when she reached home, she knew that she couldn't put off calling her friend any longer. She dialed the number Alyson had given her for the hotel where they would be staying in Hawaii.

"I'm sorry, we have no one by that name registered here," the desk clerk informed her.

"But that's not possible," Laci said. "Mrs. Spencer Donovan gave me this number."

"When were they to arrive?" the clerk asked.

Laci told him and waited while he checked.

"Apparently Mr. Donovan canceled those reservations."

Laci stood holding the phone, dumbstruck, her fear spiking. Spencer had canceled the hotel reservations? Why?

So Laci couldn't warn Alyson.

As BRIDGER HEADED out of town toward the ranch he rented outside of Old Town Whitehorse, he spotted the nursing home marquee announcing one of the resident's birthdays. It was later than usual, but still he turned into the lot.

It had become a ritual, stopping by every day to pay Pearl Cavanaugh and the other elderly Whitehorse Sewing Circle women a visit. He'd been told by the nurses that Pearl had been quite the woman before her stroke.

While her mother may have started the quilting group and possibly the adoptions, there was little doubt that Pearl Cavanaugh had been the ringleader during the time that he and Eve were adopted.

He stuck his head in Pearl's room. Her husband Titus visited every morning and early in the afternoon. Bridger made a point of making sure their paths didn't cross. He'd attempted to ask Titus about the adoption ring but had been quickly rebuked and threatened with slander. If Titus knew anything, he wasn't talking. Just like the rest of them.

Pearl was lying in bed, her blue eyes open and fixed on the ceiling.

"How are you doing today, Pearl?"

No response. But then, he hadn't expected one.

He pulled up a chair beside her bed and looked into her soft-skinned wrinkled face. It reflected years of living, and yet there was a gentle strength about her. He wished he had known her before the stroke. Guilt consumed him since he felt he was partly to blame for putting her here. If he hadn't come to Whitehorse looking for answers, maybe she wouldn't have had the stroke.

He took her frail hand. The skin was thin and pale, lifeless. Her eyes moved to him. "Remember me? Bridger Duvall. I'm one of your babies."

Did something change in her expression? He could never be sure as he told her—as he always did—about his adoptive parents, about growing up on a ranch outside of Roundup, Montana.

"I loved my parents and miss them terribly, but I still want to know who my birth mother is. From what everyone has told me about you," he continued, "you have to have known that some of the children you adopted out would come looking for their birth parents. You would have kept a record."

He thought he saw something flicker in her pale blue eyes—eyes the same exact color as her granddaughter Laci's. He was more convinced than ever that Pearl was in there, just unable to respond.

"You know who she is, don't you?" He looked down at her hand. It was cool to the touch, the skin silken and thinly lined with veins. He stroked it gently.

"How to get that information out is the problem, huh? Don't worry, I'll be here every day to see you, and one of these days you'll be able to tell me." He smiled at her. "You're going to get better."

Tears welled in her eyes, and for a moment he thought she'd squeezed his hand just a little as he placed it carefully back on the bed.

As he rose, he saw that she was no longer looking at him but behind him. He spun around expecting to see Titus in the doorway, but it was another elderly lady he'd seen around the nursing home.

The woman was tall with cropped gray hair and a permanent scowl on her face. She quickly turned and took off down the hall.

As he started after her, a nurse appeared in the doorway. "Everything all right in here? I just saw Bertie Cavanaugh take off like a shot. She wasn't bothering you, was she?"

Bridger shook his head. The nursing staff had been very kind to him. At first they'd been suspicious, but after a while seemed thankful for his visits to the patients.

"Bertie *Cavanaugh*?" he said. "Any relation to Pearl?"

"Everyone from Old Town Whitehorse is related one way or another," the nurse said with a laugh. "I think they might be second cousins through marriage."

Another elderly woman from Old Town. Had she belonged to the sewing circle? He'd have to find out. He tried not to get his hopes up. One of his first leads was a woman who was deeply involved in the illegal adoption ring, Nina Mae Cross. Unfortunately Nina Mae had Alzheimer's and was of no help at all to him, even though he continued to visit her, as well.

"See you tomorrow, Pearl," he said as he left. She was staring up at the ceiling again, but he had the strangest feeling that seeing Bertie Cavanaugh had upset her.

Or did she fear that Bertie had overheard what they'd been talking about? His adoption.

Chapter Four

Laci tried to stem her panic as she questioned the hotel clerk about the last-minute change. "Do you have any idea where Mr. and Mrs. Donovan went?" She heard the slight hesitation in the young man's tone. "It's urgent that I contact my friend. It really could be a matter of life and death."

"We're not supposed to give out that information," the clerk said, dropping his voice. "But I did overhear the conversation. He asked our manager about a hotel more out of the way. More *secluded*."

Her heart lodged in her throat. More secluded?

"I heard our manager tell him to try the Pacific Cove."

"Thank you so much. You may have

saved a life. You don't happen to have that number, do you?"

The clerk at the Pacific Cove Inn rang Mrs. Spencer Donovan's room. The phone rang three times, and Laci was debating whether she should leave a message or not when Alyson came on the line giggling.

"Aly?"

"Laci!" her friend cried in surprise. "I was so worried you wouldn't get the message."

"Message? Why? Has something happened?" Laci asked, heart pounding. Her friend sounded fine, but still Laci couldn't help the fear she heard in her own voice.

"Happened? No, silly. The message that Spencer left you about the change of lodging. He is so thoughtful. He insisted we upgrade to a place that was more romantic."

More romantic? Or just more isolated? Laci thought, barely able to breathe. She hadn't gotten any message from Spencer. Or had that been him calling earlier today? "So it's just the two of you there?"

Alyson laughed. "Of course not. It's just a little smaller hotel with a private beach."

"Then everything is all right?"

"It's amazing. Laci, I'm having the time of my life. Spencer is so wonderful. I keep pinching myself. I can't believe any of this—Hawaii, marriage, Spencer… Just a minute, he wants to say hello."

Laci swore under her breath as Alyson handed off the phone before Laci could stop her.

"Laci, hi. I wasn't sure you got my message about the hotel change. The line sounded funny. I didn't think you could hear me."

She'd heard breathing. She knew he'd been able to hear her. Or had he?

"I just wanted to thank you for everything," Spencer was saying. "Alyson and I were just talking about what a great friend you are. So great, in fact, we've made a decision." He sounded excited.

Laci held her breath.

"We're going to settle on the ranch in Old Town Whitehorse," Spencer said with a flourish. "It's definite. With my business, I can work from anywhere, and Aly's heart is set on being near you."

"I'm so glad," Laci managed to get out.

He was calling Alyson *Aly?* That's what Laci called her.

"Great, she'd hoped you would be. I'll tell her. I'm looking forward to getting to know you better. Listen, we were just heading out for some early sightseeing, but thanks again for everything. Aly says she'll talk to you soon." The line went dead.

Laci stood holding the phone, her hand shaking, her emotions running wild. Had Spencer really tried to leave her a message? Had she been wrong about hearing breathing on the line? He'd sounded so sincere on the phone. And Alyson…Aly was apparently safe, happy and having the time of her life. Not only that, the two planned to settle here.

Laci still couldn't believe it. Was it possible she'd been wrong?

She breathed a shaky sigh of relief, telling herself that everything was going to be fine. It had been the champagne mixed with a huge dose of overactive imagination. Or maybe she really was losing her mind.

After all, she'd agreed to this cook-off at Bridger Duvall's new restaurant. Clearly she couldn't trust her instincts.

She went out on the porch, needing fresh air to clear her head. She knew she should be going through her recipes for the cooking contest with Bridger's head chef tomorrow. Who had he got? Probably someone out of Bozeman. She'd eaten at several of the more elite restaurants there and knew they had some excellent chefs.

As she started to sit down in the porch swing, she noticed a square of white paper under it on the floor. Bending, she picked up a white envelope and turned it over to see in small, boxy print the words *Laci Cherry*.

Cherry? That had been her father's name, but after his death and her mother's desertion, her grandparents had adopted her and her sister Laney and given them the family name Cavanaugh.

She stared down at the envelope. No one knew her as Laci Cherry. Except maybe one person who might not know that her name had changed, she thought, her pulse pounding in her ears. That person had left Old Town Whitehorse twenty-eight years ago, when Laci was barely a year old, and had never been heard from again.

Laci's mother, Geneva Cavanaugh Cherry.

She stared down at the envelope, her fingers trembling. There was no return address, no stamp. Nothing but her former name.

She wasn't sure what frightened her more: what was inside the envelope or why someone would just leave it on her porch. Carefully she turned the small white envelope over in her fingers. How long had it been under the swing and she just hadn't noticed? She had no way of telling.

If the envelope hadn't been addressed to Laci *Cherry*, she wouldn't have thought anything about it. But this reminder from the past scared her.

If only Laney were here. Her sister would have opened it by now.

Laci looked up the road as if she might see a vehicle. There was nothing but open prairie and rolling hills for miles, no sign of life. No clue as to who might have left it.

Feeling vulnerable, as if her home had been violated, she stepped inside and sniffed the air to see if she could tell whether the person had done more than just leave the note on her porch.

She never locked her door. Few people around here ever did. She walked through the house. Nothing that she could tell had been disturbed. But that didn't mean that someone hadn't been inside.

At the small desk in the kitchen, she took out the letter opener. Making a nice clean slice, she cut open the envelope and peered inside. A single sheet of matching white paper.

You're going to feel so foolish when you read what's inside. Nothing scary. No ghosts from the past. Just someone caught in a time warp. Like Alice Miller. She often got the names of residents confused, but she was almost ninety.

Carefully, as if lifting out something fragile, Laci took the sheet of paper from the envelope and unfolded it.

She'd been hoping the paper would contain a nice note from someone in the community. A note telling her how elegant she'd looked at Alyson's wedding. Or even a thank-you for the goodies she'd been baking and taking to the nursing home.

But, of course, it was neither. Normal people mailed their letters. They didn't leave them on your porch, where you may or may not find them.

All the writing was in the center of the note. Small and boxy, just like the writing on the envelope.

I know what really happened to your mother.

A dagger of ice ran through her. She stared at the words, telling herself it was just somebody's idea of a prank. If the person really knew something, then why not come forward? And why wait nearly thirty years to do so?

She debated just tossing the note in the trash, but instead carefully put it back into the envelope, checking to make sure she hadn't missed an address or other identifying mark before putting it into the kitchen desk drawer, all the time wondering if this had something to do with that mysterious call she'd gotten before. Had someone been trying to tell her something then but decided to send her a note instead?

The one thing she wasn't going to do was

call Laney again on her honeymoon and upset her, even though Laci was sure her sister would have told her it was nothing. But then, Laney didn't like talking about their mother.

From the time Laci was small she'd always heard that her mother had packed up a few things and left town shortly after her husband had been killed in a car accident north of Old Town Whitehorse.

Apparently her mother had been so deeply in love with Russell Cherry that she hadn't been able to live with any reminders of him. Those reminders, Laci assumed, being Old Town Whitehorse and the house her parents had built for her and her husband and her children, Laney and Laci.

Laci had never understood how any mother could leave two small children, just walk out the door with little more than a photo album, a suitcase and a few dollars in her purse and never look back.

Laci had been so young that she didn't even remember her mother. While she knew now that her mother had never been back, she'd once pretended that her mother hadn't really left. That Geneva watched over her and Laney.

Like the first day of school, both sisters scrubbed clean and wearing their best dresses. What mother could miss that? Laci had walked with her head up, wanting to make her mother proud as she entered the one-room schoolhouse, positive that Geneva was hiding in the trees nearby watching her and Laney.

Other major events Laci had been sure her mother had witnessed, as well. Her daughters' birthdays, Christmas, Easter Sunday service and egg hunts, elementary, high school and college graduations.

Laci had often searched the crowd, hoping to see her mother's face, although she believed her mother was too good at hiding to ever be seen.

And while struggling with why her mother had left, why she had never shown herself, Laci had held on to her fantasy that her mother cared.

That was, until she'd returned to the house in Old Town Whitehorse. At twenty-nine, she no longer kidded herself that Geneva

Cherry was hiding behind the old barn in the distance or behind the big trees by the schoolhouse, watching over her daughters.

Geneva Cherry had left and never come back. Not for Laci's first day of school, not for her home run in Little League, not for her culinary school graduation or even Gramma Pearl's stroke.

Or had she?

BRIDGER DUVALL WASN'T altogether sure Laci would show up. She'd been pretty adamant about not wanting the job. He was counting on her love of cooking. Not just to get her to show up for their cook-off but to make her accept his job offer.

True, he had an ulterior motive. Several, in fact. He really did need a chef. Also, he liked her. And then there was the fact that she was Pearl Cavanaugh's granddaughter. It was a long shot that she'd know anything about the Whitehorse Sewing Circle's adoptions. She wasn't even born the night his parents rendezvoused with her grandmother in the Whitehorse Cemetery.

Either way, he was looking forward to

seeing her again. He'd asked around and found out that Laci had started a catering business but hadn't had the best of results since someone was poisoned at her very first event.

While the case had been solved and Laci cleared, he doubted it had helped business.

He looked up at the sound of the front door opening. She came in with a large box of supplies and a look of determination on her face, both making him grin. She'd shown up. He breathed a sigh of relief, happier to see her than he probably should have been.

"Where's your chef?" she asked as she glanced around the large commercial kitchen.

"You're looking at him," he said, smiling.

"You?" She sounded more than skeptical.

"What? You don't think cowboys can cook?"

"A can of beans over an open fire, maybe."

His smile broadened. "I hate to make you eat your words, but I can cook you under the table."

Her blue eyes sparkled. "We'll see about that, Duvall," she said, putting down her box of supplies and tying on her apron.

They cooked in a companionable silence, both lost in their work. He would catch whiffs of what she was making and turn to watch her. Her intensity surprised him. He had to reformulate his first impression of her from the wedding reception. All he'd seen was a blond airhead, more than a little flaky, upchucking her champagne.

He stepped closer to see what she was cooking up. An interesting aroma rose up from the pot, mingling with the rich, sweet scent of Laci Cavanaugh's perfume. It was more than he could stand.

"Are you trying to steal my secrets?" she asked, cutting her eyes to him.

"I have to have a bite."

She grinned and handed him a spoonful.

He couldn't believe the flavors. "It's amazing."

Her grin broadened into a blazing smile. He looked into those big blue eyes and did the worst possible thing he could do. He leaned over and kissed her. It was just a brush of their lips, a comingling of tastes and touch.

The bolt of shock that rocketed through

him wasn't just from the spark of the kiss. The moment their lips touched, Bridger knew hiring Laci Cavanaugh was out of the question.

Was he crazy? He couldn't have this woman in his kitchen. She would be too distracting. Just watching her cook was a huge turn-on since she clearly loved cooking as much as he did—and she was damned good at it. He loved the way her brows knitted when she was concentrating on slicing vegetables. Or the way she gently bit her lower lip as she melted butter.

Who would have thought someone who looked like her could cook?

Not to mention the fact that he'd completely forgotten why he'd made a point of running into her again. He hadn't even gotten around to asking her about the Whitehorse Sewing Circle and her grandmother.

Laci's cell phone rang in her purse, making them both jump back from the kiss.

"Can you get that for me?" she asked as she dusted flour off her hands, then scrutinized the buttermilk biscuits she'd made. She slid the pan into the oven and set the timer as if pretending the kiss had never happened. Or perhaps she was unaffected by it.

Her phone rang again. She shot him a look. "It's in my purse," she said, her hands white with flour.

He nodded numbly. He'd never known a woman who would let a man in her purse. Carefully he peeked into her shoulder bag, looking for the cell as it rang a third time.

The purse had several recipes torn from magazines with printed changes written in the margin. She'd already changed the recipes before she'd even tried them? The arrogance of the woman. He loved it.

He spotted the cell and snapped it open before the phone could ring again. "Hello?"

Silence.

"Hello?" he repeated.

"Who is it?" Laci called from the stove.

"Laci?" asked a female voice on the other end of the line.

"Just a minute." He handed Laci the phone. She had begun caramelizing onions on the stove as she said hello.

"Laney," she said, sounding pleased, and

smiled over at him. "It's my sister." The sister must have asked who'd answered the phone, because Laci turned her back to him and said, "Bridger Duvall." Silence, then she said, "He's opening a restaurant in White-horse... Not sure... We're here cooking... It's a long story." She laughed, then asked how things were going in Hawaii.

Bridger turned back to his own cooking, shaken by his reactions to not only the kiss but also Laci's nonreaction, if that's what it had been. He wanted to snatch the phone from her and kiss her again, only this time *really* kiss her.

Behind him, he heard Laci gasp and turned as she dropped the phone to the floor. She'd gone white as her apron.

"What is it?" he cried.

"She's dead," Laci croaked out on a sob. "She'd dead."

Bridger lunged toward Laci, catching her just an instant before she hit the floor.

A few moments later, Laci blinked her eyes open and slowly focused on the face hovering above her. A very handsome, concerned face. She sat up with a start.

"What happened?" Bridger asked. "Talk to me."

Tears filled her eyes. "She's dead."

"Who's dead?"

"Alyson."

Bridger sat back on the floor. "Spencer's Alyson?"

She nodded through her tears. "Laney just saw it on the news in Hawaii. Aly was swimming." She choked on a sob. "She drowned." She burst into gut-wrenching sobs. "I knew it. I should have stopped her."

Bridger scooted closer and took her in his arms. She leaned into him and cried for her friend and for herself. She had let this happen. It was all her fault.

Bridger held her, letting her sob her heart out, offering his shoulder and an occasional paper towel.

Finally she took a shuddering breath and sat back. He handed her another paper towel, his eyes dark with concern.

"I'm sorry about your friend," he said.

She nodded and dried her tears. She had to do something. She was one of the few people who knew the truth about Spencer Donovan.

Rising unsteadily to her feet, she looked around for her purse and car keys.

"Let me drive you home," Bridger said, joining her. "You're too upset."

"I'm not going home," she said, buoyed by growing anger and Cavanaugh determination. "I'm going to the sheriff. He needs to know the truth."

Bridger frowned. "The truth?"

"Spencer killed her."

BRIDGER STARED AT HER as he watched her search for her keys and purse. "Laci, you can't really think that Spencer would—"

"He killed her. Oh, my God, he *killed* her." She was sobbing again, mumbling how she should have done something.

"I thought you said she drowned while swimming," he reminded her as she found what she was looking for in the supply box she'd brought and turned to leave.

"I don't know the specifics," she said, shaking her head at him as if he wasn't paying attention. "I just know that he killed her and if I don't do something he'll get away with murder." She charged toward the door.

He called after her, but there was no turning a wild bull when it was seeing red. Just as there was no turning Laci Cavanaugh when her mind was made up, apparently.

All he could hope was that the sheriff would set her straight and calm her down. He sighed and looked around the kitchen, still stunned that the pretty young bride was dead and Spencer was a widower after only a few days of marriage.

It brought home how brief life could be. He'd promised himself after his mother died that he would live his to the fullest. But, of course, he hadn't. Instead he'd gone on this quest to find his birth mother.

The timer went off on the oven. He took a hot pad and pulled out the biscuits Laci had made and turned off the burner heating the onions, too worried about her to even think about food right now.

He could understand wanting someone to blame when you lost a person you loved. He just hoped that Laci came to her senses before Spencer returned.

The last thing Spencer needed at a time

like this was his bride's best friend trying to get him arrested for murder.

SHERIFF CARTER JACKSON motioned Laci into his office. She closed the door and took a seat, having pulled herself together as much as possible on the three blocks to the sheriff's department.

"I just heard about Alyson. I'm so sorry, Laci," Carter said, making her tear up again. "I know how close the two of you were growing up."

She nodded, fighting to keep from bawling again. "There is something you don't know." Her throat was so dry she had to swallow before she could continue. "Spencer killed her."

Laci had expected the sheriff to be surprised, but all he did was nod.

"Your sister called me when she lost the cell phone connection with you," he said.

"Then she told you?"

"She mentioned your suspicions," Carter said carefully. "I called the sheriff's department on the island and talked to the investigating officer. Apparently Alyson had been in the habit of going for a swim early in the morning. This day was no different. An eye-witness from the shore said it appeared she got a cramp. The witness tried to reach her, but she'd gone under by then."

Laci was shaking her head. "Where was Spencer during all this?"

"He'd gone to the room to get something," Carter said.

How convenient. She didn't believe it. "He must have given her something, drugged her or—"

"There will be an autopsy, so if there are drugs in her system, they'll find them."

She nodded, still afraid that Spencer would get away with this.

"We're all just sick about what happened."

She stood and picked up her purse. "Alyson was a strong swimmer. She was on the swim team in high school. She wouldn't have drowned unless he did something to her."

"Strong swimmers get cramps and drown, Laci."

She shook her head. "He killed her."

"Based on a look?" the sheriff said quietly.

So Laney had told him. "I know it doesn't seem like much, but his mask slipped for that instant and I saw his true feelings. I knew he was going to kill her. I should have tried harder to stop her—"

"Why would he marry her if he really had those kind of feelings toward her?"

It was the question Laci had been asking herself for two days. Alyson's family didn't have money. The ranch would be worth something but not enough to kill someone for, right?

"Laci, it was an accident," Carter said.

"I know it sounds crazy," she admitted. "But won't you please investigate Spencer Donovan?"

"The death occurred out of my jurisdiction, and as I said, it's being investigated."

She was close to tears again. "Please, at least check out his background?"

The sheriff nodded slowly. "If you'll do me a favor. Keep your suspicions to yourself?"

She nodded. "You'll let me know what you find out?"

"I promise."

BRIDGER CALLED A HALF dozen times and stopped by on his way home, but Laci's car wasn't in the drive, nor were any of the lights on inside the house.

He could imagine how it had gone with the sheriff and hoped she was all right.

Finally he called her grandfather. Titus Cavanaugh was a big, powerful man, both in stature and in his standing in this part of Montana. Bridger had butted heads with him only the one time over the adoption business and, more to the point, over his wife Pearl and her part in it.

Finally Titus had sworn on the Bible he used for his Sunday church services that he knew nothing about Bridger's birth or adoption. Bridger had believed him.

"I'm trying to find Laci," he said without preamble.

"And who might you be?" the older man asked.

"Bridger Duvall. I was with Laci today when she got the bad news about her friend Alyson. I'm worried about her."

Silence, then finally the man said, "You

can reach her at her friend McKenna Bailey's."

"Thank you, I'll do that." He hung up, wondering if Titus would have given him the information if he knew Bridger hadn't given up on finding his birth mother. Far from it.

"Hello, you've reached the Baileys. Leave a message and we'll get back to you."

Bridger hesitated, then said, "McKenna? It's Bridger Duvall. I'm trying to find Laci. I'm worried—"

"Bridger?" Laci said as she came on the line.

He breathed a sigh of relief, surprised how good it was to hear her voice. "Laci, I was worried about you."

She made a small wounded sound. "I'm okay." She didn't sound okay. She sounded miserable.

"Listen, if there is anything I can do…"

"Thanks, but there isn't anything anyone can do now," she said. "Thanks for calling, though."

He felt so helpless. "You take care of yourself."

"THE POLICE HERE ARE convinced that it was an accident," her sister said when Laci called the next day.

"Based on what?"

"An *eyewitness*," Laney said.

"I want the name of that eyewitness," Laci said.

"You aren't serious."

Laci had never been more serious in her life. "If you can't get it for me, I'll get the sheriff to help me."

"All right," Laney said. "I'll see what I can do. Laci, you're starting to worry me."

"I know her death wasn't an accident. He killed her."

"Okay, but if you're right, why? What was his motive?"

"He's sick. Maybe he didn't want to marry her. Maybe he was forced to. Maybe Alyson was pregnant."

"Laci, even if she was pregnant, Spencer didn't have to marry her. There wasn't anyone holding a shotgun to his head at the wedding, was there?"

She knew her sister was right. Still, she made a note to check back with Sheriff

Jackson about the autopsy and whether Aly had been pregnant. "What other motive could there have been? It wasn't like Alyson or her grandfather had a lot of money."

"That old ranch house and even the sizable land the Bannings owned can't be worth much in that part of Montana," Laney said. "Sweetie, I think you're wrong about this and I hate to see you accuse the man of something he didn't do based on—what?— a look? You realize that if he loved her as much as he seemed to—to everyone but you—then he is devastated right now. He just lost his wife, the woman he loved and swore the rest of his life to. And even worse, he probably feels responsible. If he hears that her best friend now suspects him of killing his wife, imagine what that would do to him. You can't go off half-cocked with this, Laci."

"I know." She had to admit those rational thoughts *had* crossed her mind in her more sane moments. "But what if *I'm* right and he's getting away with murder?"

Her sister sighed.

"I know what you're saying, but I'm not

wrong about him," Laci said stubbornly. "And I'm going to prove it."

"Laci, I really don't like the sound of this," her sister said with both reproach and fear. "If you're right about him, then he's dangerous."

"I have to find out the truth. I owe Aly that much at least."

"You couldn't have stopped her from marrying him," Laney said adamantly. "I love Nick so much there isn't anything anyone could have said to keep me from marrying him. If Spencer is the man you think he is, then on some level Alyson knew but refused to believe the truth about him."

"You think she suspected something was wrong?"

"If you're right, then, yes, I do," Laney said. "But she wouldn't have wanted to believe it. You telling her would have only cost the two of you your friendship."

Laci knew her sister was right. "Still, I wish I had tried harder to warn her."

"By doing what? Throwing yourself in front of the car after the reception? Come on, Laci, you know that wouldn't have done any good. Stop beating yourself up over this. Nothing you can do now will bring Alyson back. Let it go."

She wished she could.

"At least let it go until I get back," Laney said. "Whatever plot you're hatching can wait until next week, can't it?"

Laci leaned back, pressing the phone to her mouth as she fought tears, remembering Alyson waving from the back window of the car as it sped away, remembering how she'd said she was having the time of her life in Hawaii.

"Promise me you won't do anything rash," Laney said. "On second thought, I know you. I'm coming home early."

"No," Laci said, wiping at her tears. "You're on your honeymoon."

"I'm not unless you promise me you won't do anything until I get back."

What was a few more days? Laney was right. It could wait that long. Alyson was dead. Nothing could change that.

Just then she heard a car on the county road to the north. Out the kitchen window she saw Spencer Donovan's vehicle. She ducked back out of sight as the car seemed to slow as it passed.

Spencer was back in Old Town Whitehorse.

"Laci?" Laney asked on the other end of the line. "I want you to promise you won't do anything until I get back or I'm getting on the next plane home."

She hated fibbing to her sister, but she knew that if she didn't promise, Laney would cut her honeymoon short and do just what she was threatening.

Laci crossed her fingers and squeezed her eyes shut. "I promise."

Chapter Five

"I was just getting ready to call you," Sheriff Carter Jackson said when Laci got him on the line the next morning.

"You found something?" She couldn't help but sound hopeful. If the sheriff had discovered anything incriminating on Spencer Donovan, then there would be an investigation by professionals. Laci wasn't foolish enough to believe she could do a better job of investigating Spencer than law enforcement.

"Probably not what you were expecting," the sheriff said. "I talked to the detective on the case in Hawaii. The autopsy confirms that Alyson drowned. There were no drugs in her system. No sign of foul play."

"Was she pregnant?"

"No." He sounded surprised by the question. "Laci, Alyson's death has been ruled an accident. The case is closed."

"But what about Spencer? There has to be something in his background—"

"I ran him through our computers. Laci, the man hasn't even had a speeding ticket in years."

She couldn't believe this. "What about his business?" Alyson had led her to believe that Spencer was wealthy. That had to be a lie. "Is he really rich?"

"Rich is a relative term, but he seems to have done very well with his investment business," the sheriff said. "You aren't thinking he was after Alyson's money?"

She wasn't sure what she was thinking. Maybe that was the problem. She wasn't thinking at all—just letting her heart rule, as she'd done all her life.

She took a deep breath and let it out slowly, trying to hold herself together.

"Other than the one look you thought he gave his bride, what is it about Donovan that has you so suspicious?"

She felt tears burn her eyes. Other than a

feeling based on nothing more than a look, there wasn't anything he'd done or said that would prove him a killer. "There's really nothing you could find on him?"

"Nothing. I hope the information gives you some peace of mind," the sheriff said. He seemed to hesitate. "Spencer Donovan stopped by my office earlier. He'd heard I'd been asking about him and his business. I told him it was standard procedure in an accidental death. I'm not sure he believed me, but he was cordial enough about it. I didn't mention your name, of course."

"Thank you for running a check on him," she said, feeling even worse. Carter had to think she was a nutcase.

"Mr. Donovan told me that he's staying out at the Banning ranch down the road from you. Is that going to be a problem for you?"

"I guess not since apparently there is nothing to worry about when it comes to him," she said. "Did he mention how long he would be staying?"

"Didn't say. I would assume at least until after the funeral. He said services are planned at the old Whitehorse Cemetery tomorrow, but I imagine you already knew that."

The moment she hung up, the phone rang. It was Laney. She told her sister what the sheriff had found out.

"What is it going to take for you to accept that this man isn't a killer?" Laney asked.

She wished she knew.

"I did get the name of the eyewitness who tried to save Alyson," her sister said.

"Maybe the eyewitness was in on it," Laci said as she scrambled to find a pen and paper. "Maybe Spencer hired this guy."

Laney groaned on the other end of the line. "The eyewitness was a woman. Her name is Joanna Clemmons from Atlanta, Georgia. She was visiting Hawaii on a church conference. Sound like a hired killer to you?"

Laci wrote down the woman's name, although her enthusiasm had waned. "I'm crazy, aren't I?"

"You're just not thinking straight, sweetie," Laney said comfortingly.

"I thought for sure she might have been drugged. Or maybe pregnant and he didn't want the baby."

"You know that if Alyson had been pregnant she would have told you," Laney assured her. "You two were best friends for too many years. She always told you everything.

Did she?

Laci wasn't so sure about that as she made another promise to her sister she had no intention of keeping, fingers crossed, and got off the line.

"I need your help," Bridger said when Laci answered the phone a few minutes later. He'd called her numerous times to see how she was doing.

She always told him the same thing: that she was okay. But he could tell by her voice that she was far from okay. He just hoped now that Spencer was back in town that she didn't still think he'd killed his bride on their honeymoon.

"I need a chef," Bridger said. "I'm having a small, invitation-only sampler just to test my proposed menu for the restaurant. The problem is that I'm in over my head. I need help. I'm *desperate*."

"As flattering as that is…"

"Laci, I need *you*. And I think it's time you

got back to cooking." He could hear from her surprised intake of breath that she hadn't expected him to know that she'd been so upset she couldn't even cook.

"How did you—"

"I can't do this without you. I can drive down and pick you up—"

"No. What are you making?"

He smiled to himself, knowing once he told her, he'd have her. He rattled off his menu.

"You don't want to make that for dessert. Not with it supposed to rain this afternoon. I have a chocolate flourless torte that would be perfect." She sighed. "I'll be there in an hour. I'll stop by the store and pick up what I need to make it."

He breathed a silent sigh of relief. "I owe you."

"Yes, you do. Wait until you get my bill."

LACI STOPPED BY THE grocery store to get what she needed to make her flourless chocolate torte, grateful to have something to do. But, in truth, also looking forward to spending time with Bridger.

The local grocery was small, the aisles narrow, but she found what she needed and pushed her cart into the checkout line.

"Excuse me."

Laci heard the male voice, recognizing it at the same moment a chill raced up her spine.

"Laci?" Spencer asked from directly behind her.

She turned, afraid of what she was going to say. She'd thought about coming face-to-face with him. All she could think about was clawing out his eyes, screaming obscenities at him.

But when she saw his face, she did neither. His dark eyes were sunken with dark circles under them. He looked horrible. She hadn't expected this, and even while she told herself this could be part of his act, she felt for him and the pain she saw in his face.

"I'm so sorry about Alyson." Her words surprised her. She sounded so civil.

He nodded. "Thank you."

She turned back as the cashier announced her total. Laci's hands were shaking as she pulled the money from her purse and paid for her groceries.

"If you wait, I can help you out with those," Spencer said behind her.

"That's all right. I can manage," she said, not looking at him.

"See you around, Laci."

She stumbled from the store, shaken. Was it possible she was wrong about Spencer Donovan?

Opening her car, she put the groceries inside and, unable to help herself, glanced back toward the store.

Through the large plate-glass window she saw him at the checkout. He was paying for his groceries, but as if feeling her gaze on him, he turned in her direction.

Their gazes locked and he smiled, but the smile never met his eyes.

ONE LOOK AT HER and Bridger knew he'd done the right thing dragging Laci into town. He tossed her an apron, biting his tongue to keep from asking how she was holding up. The way her fingers trembled as she tied on the apron said it all.

Laci had left her recipes in the kitchen at his restaurant the other day. He'd tried her flourless chocolate torte, trying to read the changes she'd made in the margin.

It had turned out all right, but he really wanted to taste hers. Somehow he knew it would be better than what he'd made even following her recipe.

"What do you need me to do?" she asked, stepping to the sink to wash her hands.

"I tried your torte recipe," he confessed. "I would like to taste it after *you* make it."

She smiled over her shoulder at him, what he suspected was her first smile in days. "What makes you think mine will be better?"

"Just a feeling," he said with a laugh. Just like the feeling that he'd called her in the nick of time. He could see the grief on her face. She looked thinner, her eyes rimmed red, her face pale.

He went to work on one of the entrées and left her to it. They cooked in silence. He watched her come back to life slowly as the kitchen filled with the sweet scents of rich, creamy butter, chocolate and raspberry.

He relaxed into the pleasurable work, the only sounds that of pots and pans and wire whips and wooden spoons and the occasional ooh or aah as one of them tasted their work of art.

The kitchen was warm and safe, just as it had been when he was a child. His mother had taught him to cook. His father had taught him to ride a horse and fish.

Both of his adoptive parents were now gone. His father from a heart attack seven years ago. His mother finding peace six months ago after a long battle with cancer.

She'd given him one final gift: the truth. Since then, he'd often wondered why he hadn't known he was adopted. Or even suspected it. How was that possible?

A door opened and closed. A female voice called, "Hello?" as cowboy boot soles thumped across the wood floor of the restaurant into the kitchen at the back.

As if conjured up from his thoughts, his twin, Eve Bailey, stopped in the doorway.

"So you're really doing this," she said. Like her sisters and mother, Eve was all cowgirl. She wore jeans, boots and a western shirt. But recently he'd noticed she was wearing makeup and fixing her hair differently. He suspected it was for the same reason Sheriff Carter Jackson was spending more time down in Old Town Whitehorse. There appeared to be some old-fashioned courting going on.

Bridger was glad to see it. He'd seen the way Eve's eyes lit when the sheriff was around.

"You got the invitation for tonight, didn't you?" Bridger asked. "I reserved a table for you." He didn't add that the sheriff had already called to reserve his best table. Wouldn't it be something if the sheriff popped the question tonight?

"Hi, Laci," Eve said.

Laci had been so involved in her cooking she hadn't seemed to have heard Eve come in.

"I assume you two know each other?" Bridger asked. He and Eve were older than Laci, but both women had grown up in Old Town Whitehorse, and as small as that community was, they probably knew each other's life histories.

"Of course," Laci said and laughed before saying hello to Eve, then going back to her cooking.

Bridger was just getting to know the town and the people. He felt as though he was thirty-two years behind even though it was the only reference spot he had in his search for his birth mother.

Eve talked for a few minutes about the weather, her new horse, the price of hay. She seemed to be avoiding mentioning Alyson's death, her eyes flicking to Laci's thin back as the younger woman continued to cook.

Bridger walked Eve out to her pickup.

"Is Laci all right?" Eve asked. "You know Alyson Banning was her best friend."

He nodded. "She'll be all right. It just takes time." He could feel Eve eyeing him.

"I'm glad you stayed around," she said as they reached her truck and she started to open the driver's-side door.

"Me, too." He wanted to apologize again for being such a jerk when he'd first come to town. He'd thought Eve Bailey was in on the cover-up involving his adoption. He hadn't realized how wrong he could be.

His mother had told him about the phone call in the middle of the night. His adoptive parents had driven all the way to Whitehorse and waited in the dark, wintry cold at the cemetery. They'd almost given up when an older woman had appeared out of the snowy darkness with a bundle.

Inside had been a baby and a new birth certificate that would make them the birth parents.

Only there'd been a mix-up. They'd been given the baby boy—but the wrong birth certificate. The birth certificate was for a little girl named Eve Bailey who'd been born the same night at the same time. His fraternal twin sister.

What he and his twin had in common was their quest to find their birth mother. But unlike him, Eve believed the answer was lost forever with Pearl Cavanaugh's stroke.

"You do realize that Laci is Pearl Cavanaugh's granddaughter, I assume," Eve said.

It was eerie the way she often knew what he was thinking.

"That isn't what this is about," he said.

She cocked a brow at him, no doubt remembering how driven he'd been to find out the truth just months ago. Not that things had changed. He was just going at it differently, he told himself.

He planned to charm them with his culinary craft. Seduce them with food cooked with his love and care. Show them he wasn't going anywhere until he got the truth. And eventually he would get what he was after. He hoped.

Eve was one of them, an Old Town Whitehorse resident, and she hadn't been able to get to the truth. Was he kidding himself that staying here was the answer?

"Laci loves to cook almost as much as I do, and I needed a cook. It's that simple." He wished.

Eve was still giving him the eagle eye. "So she's working for you?"

Was she? "I hope so." It was true. The kiss aside, he needed her expertise. She'd had some good suggestions about the menu, and the woman could cook. As long as he didn't let her distract him, everything would be fine.

"Do I say break a leg or what?" Eve asked.

"Good luck will do," he said and grinned at her. "You look nice. Date?"

"Uh-huh." Eve glanced away, shy when it came to Carter.

He smiled. "Carter's a good man."

She cut her eyes to him. "You'd better get back to your cooking."

"Eve…" he said, feeling a strange lump in his throat. So many times he'd regretted telling her he had no interest in getting to know her. His own twin sister. He'd been angry.

Since then, they'd made a pact to keep their relationship a secret. At least for the time being. There hadn't been enough evidence to expose the Whitehorse Sewing Circle, and telling everyone would only open up the whole sorry mess. "I'm glad you stopped by."

LACI BREATHED IN the scents of the kitchen, glancing around, grateful that Bridger had called her to help.

Not that she didn't know what he was up to. He was too smart to make anything for dessert that could be affected by damp weather. He just knew that she needed this and had come up with an excuse to get her down here.

Still, it surprised her that this man she'd only just met knew that the one thing she needed most right now was to be cooking.

Under normal circumstances she would have balked at such obvious manipulation. But the truth was she needed to lose herself for a few hours. She was beginning to question her own sanity since from all appearances Spencer Donovan was no more a killer than she was.

And yet her instincts told her she was right. Alyson had been murdered. And she was the only one who knew the truth.

She heard Bridger come back into the kitchen as she slid the tortes into the oven and set the oven timer.

"I couldn't have done this sampler without you," he said behind her. "Thank you. You saved my life."

She nodded without turning around as she put her recipes away. She was the one who'd been saved and they both knew it. Getting ready for his invitation-only sampler night had kept her so busy she hadn't had time to agonize over Alyson's death. Or what to do about Spencer Donovan. As if there was anything to do.

She just hoped her tortes turned out. She loved cooking here with Bridger, but she'd been too aware of him this time. She just hoped she hadn't left anything out of the recipe. One thing was for sure—she couldn't take the chef job he'd offered her, even if she was tempted. She couldn't work this close to the man. And just the thought made her a little sad.

BRIDGER HAD STOPPED JUST inside the kitchen door, watching Laci as she slid the tortes into the oven and set the timer, then began putting away her recipes.

She had a dab of flour on her cheek, her face a little flushed from the heat of the kitchen, her eyes bright and shiny. He'd never seen a more beautiful, desirable woman.

For years he'd been busy running the ranch and taking care of his elderly parents. He'd told himself he hadn't had time for relationships, but the truth was he hadn't met a woman who'd interested him enough to get involved.

Until now.

He had an idea what he was getting into with Laci. She was without a doubt a walking bundle of contradictions. Underneath all that sexy blond cuteness was a talented, imaginative, intelligent woman who would have to be reckoned with. She would be a challenge for any man.

He watched her dust flour off her hands as he stepped closer. She turned to him. Her smile was his undoing. He reached to brush the dab of flour from her cheek. Her skin was warm and silken. He felt a shaft of desire shoot through him like nothing he'd ever experienced—and knew he was lost.

"LACI." HE CUPPED HER cheek with his hand, his eyes locked with hers.

She didn't dare breathe, didn't dare move, as his mouth dropped to hers. The kiss rocked her back on her heels. His arms surrounded her and pulled her closer.

She let herself go, lost in his kiss, in the

warm, sweet taste of him, in the luscious feel of being enveloped by him. A soft moan escaped her lips. There was no turning back, and she suspected Bridger knew it, as well.

"Laci?"

She wrapped her arms around Bridger's neck as he swept her up in his arms. He drew back to look into her eyes. She saw the question and answered it with a kiss as he carried her upstairs to his apartment above the restaurant.

He kicked open the bedroom door and lowered her slowly to the bed. "You sure about this?"

She'd never been so sure of anything. She smiled up at him and pulled him down as she pushed aside her vow not to jump into anything. She needed this. She needed Bridger. All her emotions were so close to the skin. She needed to be nurtured, and this felt so right. It couldn't possibly be wrong.

Bridger lowered himself beside her. She felt shy and excited all at the same time. Her heart raced and her fingers trembled as she began to unsnap his western shirt, averting her eyes from his.

He covered her hand with his, stopping her.

With one finger he lifted her chin so that their eyes met. Slowly, painstakingly, he leaned toward her and brushed a kiss across her lips.

She caught her breath as he slowly began to undress her. She ignored the little voice in her head that argued that this was too soon, that she didn't know this man, that she'd just leaped, that she would regret it... as Bridger drew her close and she melted into his arms.

A SOUND AROUSED LACI. It took her a moment, lying there in Bridger's arms, to realize what it was. The timer on the oven.

"My tortes!" she cried and jumped out of bed, throwing on her clothing as she rushed downstairs to the kitchen.

A few moments later, Bridger came down dressed in jeans and a shirt, his feet bare. He came over to where she stood.

"Wow," he said, admiring her creation. "Wow," he repeated, only this time focusing on her.

She beamed under his gaze and stepped easily into his arms for a kiss. "Wow."

He smiled at her, making her recall too well their lovemaking. It had been a healing for her, a need that was tied up in her grief over her best friend's death, in her sense of loss.

"Your guests will be arriving in less than three hours," she said.

He nodded and sighed. "Laci—"

She touched a finger to his lips, afraid of what he might say. Her eyes locked with his and the kitchen suddenly felt much too hot. He was going to kiss her again, and she feared neither of them would remember dinner—or his guests—if he did.

"Congratulations!"

Bridger jerked back, swinging around.

Laci felt her heart plummet—not just from the disappointment of the almost kiss—but from the recognition of the male voice.

Spencer Donovan burst through the kitchen doors and froze. She pressed herself into the counter, trying to make herself invisible. Just the sound of the man's voice stole her breath and sent her heart pounding in her ears.

"You always said you were going to open a restaurant someday," Spencer was saying as the two men shook hands. "I just never imagined it would be in Whitehorse, Montana."

Spencer and Bridger knew each other? Had known each other before the wedding? The realization was an arrow to her heart. She'd just assumed Bridger had been at the wedding for the bride since he lived in Old Town Whitehorse—not there on groom's side.

She must have let out a gasp at Spencer's words. He peered around Bridger and saw her. His expression changed instantly. She saw something flicker in his gaze.

"Thanks," Bridger said, drawing Spencer's attention away from her. "I never thought my first restaurant would be in Whitehorse, either. Spence, I'm so sorry about Alyson."

Spencer only nodded, looking upset. "Well, I just had to stop in and congratulate you. I couldn't miss tonight—not when I know how much it must mean to you. Even when we were kids you always talked about opening your own restaurant."

Laci felt sick. All she wanted to do was flee. But she couldn't move, couldn't breathe.

Spencer should have been in mourning, but here he was out on the town. She knew she wasn't being fair. The man had a right to eat. But it ticked her off that he looked better than he had at the supermarket earlier. His tan seemed more prominent, and he was dressed up in jeans and a sports jacket over a button-up shirt. His gaze shifted to Laci. She looked into his dark eyes and felt as if she were drowning in a deep, dark, bottom-less well.

"Well, I should go," Spencer said and shook Bridger's hand again, slapping him on the shoulder. He gave Laci a nod and was gone.

She gasped for air, grabbing hold of the counter for support. "*You two know each other?*" she demanded the moment Spencer was out of earshot.

Bridger looked at her as if worried about her sanity. "You saw me at the wedding."

"But I had no idea you were there as *his* guest."

"I thought you knew. Spencer and I are both from Roundup."

She hadn't known. But she should have. She'd just assumed because Bridger lived in Old Town Whitehorse that he'd been Alyson's guest. The entire community was always invited to every event, whether it was a wedding, a baby shower or a birthday.

"You should have told me he was your friend."

"We're not exactly friends," Bridger said. "I hadn't seen him in years."

She groaned. "He certainly sounded like your friend. Why did you let me go on about him being a killer without telling me about your friendship?"

"Laci, I knew you were in shock and upset. I didn't really take what you were saying seriously."

She couldn't believe the man was capable of actually making her more angry. "*You didn't take me seriously?*"

"What you were *saying* seriously."

She threw her hands up in the air, almost

too exasperated to speak. "You saw him just now. Did he look like a man who is grieving?" she demanded.

"I know you're upset about the death of your friend, but you can't believe he purposefully killed his wife. Why would he do that?"

Admittedly that part didn't make any sense, especially given what the sheriff had told her. Spencer Donovan appeared to be an upstanding citizen. But appearances, as they say, could be deceiving.

"I don't know why he killed her, just that he did," she said, her chin going up in determination. "But I'm going to find out." She took off her apron and tossed it down.

"Laci—"

"You should have told me you were *his* friend."

"I told you—we aren't—"

"Do not say you aren't friends again. You were at his wedding as *his* guest."

"Only because we ran into each other in Whitewater a few weeks before the wedding. Before that, I hadn't seen Spencer in years."

She waved that off, wondering why he was trying to hide the fact that they were friends. Probably just to get her to work for him. She tried not to think about their lovemaking. Was that also to get her to cook with him?

"Come on, Laci," Bridger said as she picked up her purse and keys to leave. "I'm sorry he upset you. I really was enjoying having you here."

She could see that he wished they could go back to where they'd been earlier. About to kiss—and probably make love again. What made it worse was that so did she. "I have to go."

He looked as if he was trying to think of something to say to get her stay. But maybe he realized there was nothing he could say at this point.

She wasn't sure what made her more angry: the fact that he'd failed to tell her he and Spencer Donovan were friends, or that he didn't trust her instincts about Spencer after what they'd shared.

She gave him one last look before stalking out. The look felt filled with regret as well as anger that she had to leave this kitchen and him and, maybe worse, that there wouldn't be an encore to the kiss. Or the lovemaking.

Outside, she opened her car door and started to get in when she saw it. A single long-stemmed yellow rose. She stared at the flower, uncomprehending. Bridger hadn't put it there. When would he have? But who else would give her a rose?

She looked around, seeing no one. It had to have been Bridger, but she liked to think he was too imaginative in the kitchen to resort to flowers, the oldest cliché in the world. That he would have given her a perfect petit four that he'd baked and decorated.

Unless, of course, she didn't know him as well as she thought she did. She sighed and tossed the rose onto the passenger seat, reminding herself that she hadn't seen his friendship with Spencer coming, so clearly she didn't know Bridger as well as she'd thought.

The car smelled sickeningly sweet. She glanced over at the rose as she started the engine, feeling guilty for her lack of gratitude. Someone had left her a rose, no doubt as a nice gesture. So why did the mere sight of it make her feel queasy?

A FEW MILES DOWN THE road, she rolled down her window and tossed the rose out, feeling terrible and yet relieved to have it gone.

She hated to think what her sister would say about her throwing away a gift. Fortunately Laney was in Hawaii and would never know. Otherwise, Laci feared that this might be seen as just more irrational behavior on her part.

Everyone else thought Spencer was just who he appeared to be. All the evidence backed it up. And surely no one would see a rose as a threat. Or Bridger's friendship with Spencer as a betrayal.

She knew she wasn't being fair to Bridger. But she couldn't help how she felt. She was so lost in her mix of emotions that it didn't even register that she was being followed until she was almost to Old Town.

She glanced in her rearview mirror and

saw the headlights, belatedly aware that the car had been back there ever since she'd left Whitehorse.

Her heart began to pound as she drove through the near ghost town, past the school, the community center, the old Cherry house. There was no moon tonight, no stars peeking out of the low cloud cover. The sharp black lines of the house were etched against the dark sky. She felt a shiver as she thought of the note she'd been left about her mother. Had the same person left the rose?

Down the county road, she swung into her drive, anxious to get home, hoping there would be no more presents, no more surprises tonight. She'd been so happy earlier, so fulfilled in Bridger's big kitchen. And in his bed. She had loved working with him. The thought made her feel even worse since they wouldn't be working together again. Or making love again.

As she parked in front of the house, she realized she hadn't thought to leave a light on when she'd left. The place was cloaked in darkness. She cut the car lights and engine but didn't get out.

She waited, hoping she was wrong about the car following her. Bridger wouldn't have followed her. He couldn't have left the restaurant, not with guests coming.

The car's headlights came down the county road, the driver seeming to slow. She slid down a little in her seat, hunkering in the dark car and holding her breath, fearing the car would turn into her lane. But it went on past and took the next road—the one to the Banning ranch house.

Spencer!

She sat, gripping the steering wheel, her heart a bass drum in her chest as she fought to catch her breath. Rational thought argued that he hadn't followed her. That he'd just been going home himself.

But she knew. Just as she knew that he was responsible for Alyson's death. Spencer Donovan hadn't just followed her home, he wanted her to know that he'd followed her and was close by. And that there was nothing she could do about that any more than she could prove he was a killer.

She let out a cry of frustration as she opened her car door and raced up the porch steps. She stumbled and almost went down. Otherwise, she might not have heard the scuttling sound of something sliding across the porch floor as she caught herself.

She unlocked the front door, reached in and turned on the porch light, already knowing what she was going to find on her porch floor. A small white envelope. Exactly like the last one, right down to the two neatly hand-printed words: *Laci Cherry*.

Chapter Six

The weather in Old Town Whitehorse could—and did—change in a heartbeat. The next morning the air was cool and crisp, the sky a crystalline blue. Every day was a gift since it wouldn't be long before winter set in with below-zero freezing temperatures and snow often accompanied by howling winds.

The one thing that never changed was the speed and intensity of the gossip in the community.

The Old Town Whitehorse grapevine was as dependable as death and taxes. And this bright fall morning it hummed with the news du jour leaving everyone for miles shocked.

Word that Violet Evans might soon be released from the criminally insane unit of the Montana state mental hospital was the talk of the town.

The Whitehorse Sewing Circle was no exception.

"Why, that woman has always been crazy," whispered Muriel Brown, who probably knew crazy better than most. She took a few stitches before she added, "Do you remember when she was about eleven? That fire at the school?"

"There was no proof Violet was responsible for that," Alice Miller pointed out with a frown. Violet Evans was now being blamed for everything that had happened in Whitehorse from the time she could walk.

"How about the summer that all the cats in the neighborhood started disappearing," whispered Ella Cavanaugh. "I told you that Violet Evans was behind it. I saw her pulling her little red wagon up the road, just grinning like the cat that ate the canary. She had a dirty old blanket over whatever was inside that wagon. I should have stopped that girl right there." Ella shuddered. "She always gave me a bad feeling, that one."

"If Pearl was here, she wouldn't allow this kind of talk," Alice Miller said pointedly.

"Well, Pearl isn't here," Muriel snapped. "But Violet Evans will be soon." She lifted a brow. "She and her mother might both be back here sitting across from us. How do you feel about that?"

Alice pursed her lips but said nothing. Everyone had been quite pleased that Arlene Evans had announced she was too busy with her Internet dating service to quilt for a while.

"I just think it's shameful the way her mother tried to marry her off," Corky Mathews said in an attempt to still the ruffled feathers. "All the humiliation that poor child went through, it's no wonder she had bad feelings toward her mother."

"Bad feelings?" snapped Muriel. "The *poor* child tried to kill her mother!"

"Who hasn't wanted to kill Arlene?" Shirley Keen shot back with a laugh.

No one could argue that Arlene wasn't a bone of contention in Whitehorse. Just as no one would have been one bit sorry if Arlene took that bunch of bad seeds of hers and left the state.

"Have you seen her *son* lately?" Shirley asked, glancing toward Helene Merchant, who had brought the news of Violet's imminent release.

"Now there is the scary one of that family," Helene said. "Bo Evans, mark my words, is a psycho killer in the making. Have you seen how long his hair is? And you know Floyd left Arlene. I heard she leased the land. What else could she do? It wasn't like that boy of hers was going to run the place."

"I saw him hanging out by the old Cherry house the other night," Corky said. "I've seen lights in that place again."

"Probably because the house is haunted," Helene said with a shiver.

"I saw Bo once trying to break out the rest of the upstairs windows in that house," Corky said.

"I know he's the one who threw that rock through my window two years ago," Helene said. "He's always been a bad seed."

"It's Charlotte Evans who scares me," piped up the small voice of the elderly Pamela Chambers.

"I heard Charlotte got fired from her nail job in town and hasn't even looked for another one," Muriel chimed in.

"So they're all going to be in that house again," Ella said. "You know it's just a matter of time before something tragic happens out there."

"Will probably end up killing each other," Helene said.

They all nodded as if that wouldn't be such a bad thing.

"Just so long as they never let that Violet out of the mental hospital," Muriel said.

The talk turned then to Alyson Banning Donovan's funeral later that morning and what a tragedy it was.

"That poor man," Alice said of Spencer Donovan.

"I wonder what he'll do now. Can't imagine him staying," Helene said.

The women stitched for a few moments in silence, then began to plan for the Old Town Whitehorse Christmas bazaar just weeks away and what crafts and food everyone was going to bring.

BRIDGER WAS IN THE kitchen at the restaurant when Spencer stopped in. Last night, the test run had been a huge success. Especially

Laci's torte. Bridger had called to tell her, even though it had been late. He'd had to leave a message on her machine, suspecting she was there but didn't want to take his call.

He'd thought about trying to explain how it was between him and Spencer, but the story was too long and involved to leave on an answering machine. Not to mention he knew he'd be wasting his breath. Laci had no reason to believe him. Especially with Spencer acting as if they were long-lost friends.

But, damn, Bridger felt she should have given him the benefit of the doubt. Hadn't what happened between them meant anything to her?

Damn it. Just his luck to fall for a woman who was impossible. Couldn't Laci see that? Why would Spencer kill his wife on their honeymoon? It made no sense.

Bridger glanced around the kitchen. He had a ton of work to do if he hoped to open before Christmas. But he couldn't get Laci out of his mind.

As Spencer walked into the restaurant kitchen, Bridger saw him look around as if expecting Laci would be there. Is that why he'd stopped by? It gave Bridger more than an uncomfortable feeling. Had Spencer heard about Laci's suspicions and her determination to prove him a killer?

"I'm sorry if I messed things up for you yesterday evening at your opening by stopping by like that," Spencer said.

"No, it was fine. It wasn't my opening. I just wanted to get a response from the community as to what I planned to serve, so I did a sampler night," Bridger said, realizing he sounded nervous. Realizing also that he hadn't invited Spencer. Did Spencer feel slighted?

Spencer was looking at him funny. Or was it his imagination? "I didn't mean about the restaurant. I meant about you and Laci Cavanaugh. I saw her leave not long after I did."

Spencer had hung around outside long enough to see Laci leave?

"You should have a bell on that kitchen door so you'll know if you're about to be interrupted."

"It wasn't like that. Laci's a chef. She's

been helping me with some ideas for dishes for the restaurant." Why was he lying about his feelings for her to Spencer?

"Sure, whatever you say. You two looked good together. I hated interrupting your kiss."

Bridger just wished Spencer would get to why he'd come by. "How are you holding up?" Bridger asked pointedly, remembering what Laci had said about the man's apparent lack of grief last night. "I would have invited you to the sampler last night, but I thought you wouldn't be interested in socializing yet."

Spencer gave him a look as if to say he had been doing fine until Bridger had brought it up again. "I'll never get over Aly's death. I blame myself. I should never have let her swim alone like that. But she was such a strong swimmer and she enjoyed it so much…."

"I know how hard it must be," Bridger said, not knowing but feeling chastised. He told himself that every person grieved in his own way. Part of him still hadn't dealt with the past, and he knew it.

"I just take it a day at a time," Spencer said, moving around the kitchen, picking up utensils and putting them down as if nervous.

Not half as nervous as he was making Bridger. What was this visit about? *Something*. He knew Spencer well enough to know that the man hadn't just dropped in. Spencer always made him feel guilty. For not keeping in touch all these years. For not feeling close to Spencer. After everything that had happened during their childhood, shouldn't he feel something more than a resentful indebtedness?

"It's probably wise taking it a day at a time," Bridger said.

Spencer turned to look over his shoulder at him. "I try not to think about it," he said pointedly. "It's bad enough I'll have to live with the memory the rest of my life. Actually, that's why I'm here."

Finally, Bridger thought, remembering how he had wanted to turn down Spencer's wedding invitation but had felt trapped into going. Just as he felt on the spot now.

"I was hoping you'd go to the funeral with

me this morning," Spencer said. "I don't know anyone else in town. I mean, I've met people, but you're the only person I really *know.*"

Bridger felt the full weight of their past press down on him. He knew at that moment why he'd avoided Spencer for years, resenting the bond between them, hating the guilt as well as the shame.

But Spencer was wrong about one thing. He *didn't* know Bridger, hadn't even when they were kids. Sure as hell didn't know him after all this time.

Nor could Bridger be sure he knew Spencer, he reminded himself, thinking of Laci's suspicions.

"I wouldn't ask, but I'm feeling a little desperate," Spencer said. "I guess it's the grief, but I feel like I'm never going to be allowed to be happy and that Alyson's death is all my fault because of my rotten luck."

"That's crazy."

Spencer nodded, avoiding his gaze. "Maybe."

Bridger tried to come up with an excuse not to go to the funeral with Spencer, but in the end he had no choice. He'd planned on attending the funeral anyway for Laci. He couldn't very well tell Spencer he couldn't make it and then show up.

"I really would appreciate it," Spencer said. "I'm having a tough time, but with you there, well, it will make things a little easier."

"Sure." What else could he say? He thought of Laci and groaned inwardly. She would just see this as more betrayal, but there was nothing he could do about that now.

"Great," Spencer said, giving him a slap on the shoulder. "I knew I could count on you, old buddy."

The *old buddy* grated and only made Bridger feel worse. They discussed where and when to meet and Spencer left. Bridger reminded himself that Spencer would be leaving town soon, probably right after the funeral, and it would be the last he might ever see of him. But he feared it would be too late to patch things up with Laci.

LACI WOKE WITH A terrible headache. She hadn't slept well last night. At three, she'd gotten up and taken something to help her sleep. And now she'd overslept and felt horrible.

Unfortunately she was also still spooked just knowing Spencer Donovan was only down the road from her. She didn't like being afraid. And knew she might not even have a reason—if she was wrong about him. That was why she had to find out the truth, she'd realized on waking. She wouldn't be able to rest until she did.

Doing something also kept her mind off Bridger. She felt sick as she realized she'd done exactly what she'd sworn not to. She'd leaped before she'd looked. She didn't know Bridger. Wouldn't have guessed that he was a friend of Spencer Donovan's. What else didn't she know about him?

She picked up the phone and dialed information in Atlanta for a Joanna Clemmons, telling herself that the woman probably wouldn't be listed or might still be in Hawaii.

The automated voice on the line gave her the number. Laci dialed, holding her breath.

A woman with a Southern accent answered on the second ring.

"Joanna Clemmons?" Laci asked, then rushed on before the woman thought it was a telemarketer calling. "I'm calling about the drowning of Alyson Donovan in Hawaii. I understand you were the only eyewitness?"

"Yes," the woman said cautiously.

"My name is Laci Cavanaugh. Alyson was my best friend."

"Oh, I'm so sorry," Joanna Clemmons said quickly.

"Can you tell me what happened?"

"Well, I already told the police, but I had seen your friend swimming in the morning while I was at the hotel. She apparently loved the water."

"Yes," Laci said, closing her eyes to fight back the tears.

"This particular morning the surf was rough. I just caught glimpses of her out there and then suddenly I realized she was in trouble. I heard her scream for help and then she went under as if struggling."

"Where was her husband?"

"He was in their cabana but came running out to the water after her scream for help."

"Did he try to save her?" Laci asked and held her breath.

"He did."

Laci heard the hesitation in the woman's voice. "But?"

"He seemed to hesitate. I got the impression he didn't swim."

"But he finally went in the water?"

"Yes. Apparently he isn't a very good swimmer. I was afraid he was going to drown before the hotel staff could get him to shore after… He was so devastated."

Sure he was. "There wasn't a lifeguard on duty at the hotel?"

"Not on the beach."

Laci wondered if that was another reason Spencer had chosen that particular hotel.

"I am so sorry for your loss," Joanna said.

"Thank you. I appreciate hearing what happened." Laci hung up, blinded by tears of pain and fury. She wasn't sure how Spencer had done it, but she was all the more convinced that Alyson's drowning was no accident.

As Laci got out of bed, she knocked the white envelope off her nightstand. It fluttered to the floor, landing faceup. The words *Laci Cherry* stared up at her.

She let out a curse at the sight of the envelope. She'd forgotten about it, she'd been so upset about Spencer. Had he really followed her home last night, as she suspected? He'd definitely driven by slowly, as if watching her from the darkness of his car.

She shivered at the memory. He frightened her much more than some stupid note, she told herself as she picked up the unopened envelope.

The sender made her angry. She was tempted to throw the stupid thing away without opening it. If someone had something to tell her, then she wished they'd just do it and get it over with. Why the games?

Was it possible Spencer was behind this? Alyson might have told him about Laci's family. How she and Aly were both raised by grandparents—and why. So Spencer would know about Laci's father and mother. And about her grandfather and grandmother Cherry.

She shook her head at her own paranoia. Spencer had been in Hawaii with Alyson when the first envelope was left on her porch. Even she was beginning to wonder if she wasn't making a case against him because she wanted someone to blame for her friend's death.

If only she hadn't seen that look he'd given Alyson at the reception.

Angrily she ripped open the envelope, pulled out the sheet of paper and braced herself for what she would find printed on the page.

But nothing could have prepared her for what was written there.

Your mother never left town.

Chapter Seven

"Where did you get these?" Sheriff Carter Jackson asked, picking up the two small white envelopes Laci had put in separate plastic bags.

"They were left for me on the porch at the house," she told him.

He nodded and, after pulling on a pair of latex gloves at her insistence, opened the bag she'd marked "No. 1."

His gaze rose from the note to her.

Laci said nothing, waiting for him to read the second one.

"Any idea who might be sending these to you?" he asked after he'd read them.

She shook her head. "I've always been told that my mother left town because she couldn't live without my father. Is there something else I should know?"

Carter put the notes back in the envelopes. "That's what I've always heard, as well. After you called and said you were bringing in the notes, I did give Todd Hamilton a call. He was sheriff when your mother left. He's living over in Great Falls now with his daughter."

"So the sheriff was called in?" This was news.

"Apparently your mother left a note saying she needed some time alone, but when your grandparents didn't hear from her after a couple of weeks, they filed a missing-person's report with him."

Her mother had left a note? "She didn't say where she was going?"

"No. The fact that she took a few personal items with her indicated to the sheriff that she'd left of her own free will."

Laci didn't like the bad feeling she was getting. "Wasn't he concerned when she didn't turn up?"

"The missing-person's report went out across the country, but while there were some unconfirmed sightings, she was never located." The sheriff seemed to hesitate. "It was assumed she didn't want to be found."

"No one suspected foul play?"

"There was no reason to. Your mother was young, her husband had just died, she had two small children…." He shrugged. "That's a lot for anyone to face, let alone someone her age."

Laci shook her head, not wanting to believe her mother had just run out on them because she wasn't strong enough. How could the daughter of Pearl and Titus Cavanaugh have been a quitter? It went against the genes.

And yet Laci had considered quitting after all the evidence pointed to Spencer Donovan's innocence even though her instincts told her he was a murderer.

"Thank you for the information," she told the sheriff as she got up to leave.

He rose from his chair. "Let me know if you get any more notes. I'll run these for prints and get back to you. In the meantime, I wouldn't put much stock in them. If someone knew where your mother was, they would have come forward before this, don't you think?"

Unless for some reason they couldn't.

Laci was lost in thoughts of her mother and the person who was sending her the notes as she drove to the post office to pick up her mail. She said hello to several people she passed. The post office was where you eventually ran into everyone from the county since Whitehorse didn't have door-to-door mail service, and even with rural delivery out in Old Town Whitehorse, packages were often held at the P.O. to be picked up.

As she was coming out, she suddenly sensed someone watching her. She shivered as she looked up but saw no one. Walking to her car, though, she couldn't shake the feeling. It wasn't until she started to open her car door that she saw him.

Spencer Donovan. He was sitting in the coffee shop across from the post office. He acted as if he'd just noticed her and nodded brusquely before turning away.

Laci found herself shaking as she pulled open her door, convinced he'd been following her, would know she'd gone to the sheriff's office this morning. Only he wouldn't know that this time it had been about her mother and not him.

As she opened her car door, she caught the sweet-sick smell of the yellow rose before she saw it lying on her driver's-side seat.

MILK RIVER EXAMINER reporter Glen Whitaker walked past the new restaurant and peered in the window. He'd been trying to get an interview with Bridger Duvall since he'd moved to the area.

Other than a brief article about Duvall's business license to open the restaurant, he'd found out little about the man and had no luck in getting Duvall to talk to him.

Which Glen found as strange as Bridger Duvall himself. Most anyone who opened a business wanted the free publicity of a feature article in the newspaper.

But then, apparently Bridger Duvall wasn't most people. First he'd rented the old McAllister place in Old Town and now he was starting a business in Whitehorse. There was talk that he would be moving permanently into the apartment over the restaurant since the old McAllister place had sold to a former detective and her husband.

On top of that, no one knew anything

about Bridger Duvall—where he'd come from or, maybe more important, why he was here.

But apparently he had some connection to that man who'd married Alyson Banning—Spencer Donovan. Glen had also been trying to get an interview with the widower, with about the same luck as he'd had with Duvall. He'd heard that the two men were friends. Interesting.

Also interesting was a brunette woman Glen had seen several times—right after he'd seen Spencer Donovan. The woman had clearly not wanted to be seen. Glen had gotten the impression that she was following Donovan. To meet up with him later?

Glen had a nose for news that he was glad to realize he hadn't lost. Since moving to Whitehorse he hadn't covered much of interest. But he sensed that there was definitely a story in either Spencer Donovan, his recently drowned wife or this brunette. Or at least in Bridger Duvall and what he was up to.

Both men were unknowns and new to the community. Glen felt it was his job to find out as much about both and let residents know who was living right next door to them. Not to mention the fact that he was nosier than hell.

He had to drive down to Old Town Whitehorse to do a story for the newspaper on Alice Miller's ninetieth birthday this afternoon and Alyson Banning's funeral this morning. He'd take a few photos and—who knew—maybe catch Spencer Donovan off guard and get an interview. He was very curious about the man's wife's death.

Glen hadn't been in Old Town Whitehorse in months, not since he'd been beaten and left beside the road. It had been a humiliating experience, one he tried not to think about. An Old Town Whitehorse teenager had been caught and was supposedly behind a series of men bashings, but Glen still felt strange whenever he had to do a story down that way.

As he was walking to his car, he saw Bridger Duvall pull up and go into the restaurant with a large box of supplies.

Glen watched him, thinking the man must be anxious to get his restaurant open since he'd been working day and night on the place. It gave Glen an idea. While he was down in Whitehorse maybe he'd stop by the old McAllister place and have a look around before Duvall moved out. What would it hurt?

THE WHITEHORSE CEMETERY perched on a small hill overlooking what was left of Old Town. Trees had been planted in and around the clusters of gravestones.

Bridger stood next to Spencer beside the open grave, his hat in his hand. A breeze sent what was left of the leaves showering down from the trees, scattering them around the weathered gravestones. The sun slanted down through the branches as Titus Cavanaugh, the patriarch of Whitehorse, stood next to Spencer, his Bible in both hands, and waited for everyone to gather around the coffin.

Where was Laci? He hadn't seen her, but there were too many mourners for him to find her in the crowd without being obvious. He knew she had to be there. He just wished he was with her, feeling awkward and conspicuous standing next to Spencer.

Like Spencer, he was an outsider. He hadn't even known Alyson. Hell, he couldn't even say he knew Spencer after all these years.

Bridger could feel eyes on him, feel the curiosity and the animosity. Old Town Whitehorse was a close-knit community. The members of the Whitehorse Sewing Circle had thrown up a silent barrier to keep him out.

"They protect their own," Eve had told him. "The Whitehorse Sewing Circle is impenetrable. They're worse than a secret society when it comes to keeping secrets. If they wouldn't tell me, there isn't a chance in hell they will tell you."

He was finding that out. Just as he was sure many of them knew he visited Pearl Cavanaugh and the other elderly former members of the sewing circle at the nursing home.

"It is on the saddest occasion that we are gathered here today," Titus began. "We come to say goodbye to Alyson Banning Donovan. Only days ago, we gathered in the community center to marry this couple and give our blessing to their marriage."

As Titus continued, Bridger scanned the crowd for Laci. No sign of her. He tried not to worry. One woman in the crowd caught his eye. She had dark hair and eyes…and was about the right age to have given birth to twins thirty-two years ago.

A lot of women in the county could have been his and Eve's birth mother. But more than likely he and Eve had been brought in from somewhere else. Did someone in this town know the truth? Was that person watching him now, worried that he would find out who they were?

He felt an intent gaze on him and looked up to see the reporter from the *Milk River Examiner*, Glen Whitaker, watching him with open speculation. Bridger knew exactly what the man wanted. He'd been dogging him ever since he'd moved to Whitehorse, but more so since the death of Dr. Holloway.

The man could be a problem. Bridger knew he had to watch his step. At one point, he thought about telling Glen Whitaker the whole story, but he knew enough about Old Town Whitehorse to know that exposing the Whitehorse Sewing Circle would only make the residents close ranks even tighter around their secrets. Add to that, there was no proof.

And if there were records on the babies somewhere—which Bridger prayed there were—then he didn't want to do anything that might make those involved destroy them to protect themselves and the adopted babies.

The wind moaned in the tops of the nearly bare branches of the trees and scuttled along on the ground, kicking up fallen leaves as Titus read a short passage from the Bible, then asked if anyone had something they wanted to say.

"Titus suggested a graveside ceremony," Spencer had told him when they'd met at the cemetery. "Too many people for the community center. Better this way. Short and sweet. It's what Alyson would have wanted."

Or what Spencer wanted, Bridger thought. How well had Spencer known his wife? Bridger couldn't imagine that the subject of funerals had ever come up when they were dating. And they hadn't dated long before they'd decided to get married, from what he'd gathered.

Such a big decision to be made so

quickly. He believed, as his adopted parents had, that marriage was for life. Maybe that is why he'd never met anyone he wanted to spend the rest of his life with—even before he found out he wasn't who he'd thought for the last thirty-two years.

Several residents stepped forward to say how badly they felt for Spencer, how much they missed Alyson. Bridger glanced down the hillside and spotted Laci at the edge of the trees. She wore all black, including a black hat that hid most of her blond hair.

Even from a distance he could see that her blue eyes were rimmed in red from crying. He wished he could go to her. Wished she'd give him a chance to explain his relationship with Spencer along with why he'd been at the wedding, why he was standing here with him now.

Beside him, Spencer followed his gaze to Laci, then shifted his feet and began to cry quietly, his body jerking spasmodically as if fighting to hold back his tears.

Bridger saw Laci's expression. Her face was set in fury and disgust as she watched Spencer, clearly not believing his grief.

Titus closed his Bible and said, "Let us pray."

Bridger bowed his head in prayer, unable to shake the bad feeling he had.

"Amen." He looked up to find Laci gone. A sliver of worry burrowed under his skin. If he knew Laci—and he was beginning to—then she wouldn't stop until she exposed Spencer for the man she believed him to be. A cold-blooded killer. But what worried Bridger more was even the slightest chance that she could be right.

LACI WAS HALFWAY DOWN the hillside when Bridger caught up with her.

"Hold up," he said, sounding out of breath. "Hey, you all right?" He must have realized how stupid his question was. "Of course you aren't all right. Sorry."

She watched him look down at his dress boots, then up at her as if at a loss for words.

"I've missed you," he said. "I was hoping you'd come back to the restaurant. I need you."

She felt her heart deflate. He just needed a *chef.* "I told you—I have my own catering business."

"Laci, please, can't we at least talk about this?"

"There's nothing to talk about," she said and glanced past him to where residents were offering their condolences. Spencer, as if sensing her gaze, glanced up and looked right at her.

"Come on, Laci, don't let Spencer come between us." Bridger pulled off his Stetson and raked a hand through his hair. "And don't even try to tell me there isn't anything more between us than cooking."

She couldn't, even if she wanted to. They'd been amazing together. How could she tell him that she'd broken her vow to herself and—worse—as hard as she'd tried, she didn't regret what she'd done. In fact, all she could think about was being in his arms again.

"I have to go." She met his gaze. "I just need to sort some things out."

"Tell me this doesn't have anything to do with Spencer Donovan," Bridger said.

She couldn't, so she didn't even try. Turning, she walked toward her car feeling Spencer's eyes boring into her back like a bullet.

"*Laci.*" Bridger caught up to her. "We have to talk about this."

"He's watching us right now," she said. "He's worried that I'm going to make trouble."

"He's not the only one. You have to let me explain about Spencer. I hate to see you so upset and angry."

"You don't believe he killed my friend," she said, daring him to deny it.

"No, I'm sorry, but I don't."

She started to turn away from him, but his words stopped her.

"I'm worried about *you.*"

"If he isn't dangerous, then what's to worry about?"

"What you're doing to yourself. This anger you have toward Spencer. You have no evidence that he had anything to do with his wife's death."

"Not yet."

He pulled off his western hat and raked a hand through his hair again. His hair was dark and thick, a little long at the neck. His skin was lightly tanned. There were tiny crow's-feet around his dark eyes. It caught her off guard just how sexy this man was, she noted now with irritation.

"This is what I'm talking about," he said. "This vendetta you're on. I know what it's like to get on a quest and lose sight of everything else. What if you're wrong about Spencer?"

"And what if *you* are?" She shook her head, tears burning her eyes. Bridger was the one person she needed to understand, but he was blinded by his friendship with Spencer. "I can't let him get away with murdering Alyson." She stole a glance past Bridger. Spencer was talking to her grandfather, but his gaze kept returning to her and Bridger. "If he's innocent, then why doesn't he like me talking to you?"

"I don't give a damn what he likes," Bridger snapped, his anger surprising her.

"Then why do you keep defending him?" she demanded. "You said yourself you hadn't seen him in years. How could you possibly know what he's capable of anymore?" She shook her head. Why *was* he defending Spencer? "What aren't you telling me?" Something. She could feel it.

When he didn't answer, she turned to leave.

He grabbed her arm. "Spencer saved my life."

She turned to stare at him, stunned.

He let go of her and sighed. "I told you we grew up together in Roundup, Montana. What I didn't tell you was that we were crossing a frozen creek near town one day and I fell in and went under the ice. Spencer jumped in after me, managed to break through the ice downstream and save my life. It almost cost him his."

She finally understood his loyalty to Spencer. "You were kids. He's changed," she said quietly, seeing the weight of this debt on Bridger. "I talked to the eyewitness. Spencer stood on the beach and let Alyson drown. By the time he went into the water it was too late."

Bridger looked away for a moment. "There's something you have to understand. Spencer got caught under the ice after he saved me. I called for help, but by the time we got him out he was unresponsive. While the EMTs were able to revive him, from that day on he was terrified of water."

"Then why a honeymoon in Hawaii?"

"When I ran into Spencer and he told me he was getting married and invited me to the wedding, he told me that Alyson had her heart set on Hawaii—and you said yourself she loved to swim. He said he didn't have the heart to tell her Hawaii was the last place he wanted to go."

Laci couldn't believe the way Spencer had set it up even before the wedding. "I have to go."

"Laci—"

"Did you know he's been following me?"

"What?"

"Every time I turn around, he's there. And that's not all. He's been leaving me presents."

"Presents?"

She saw the disbelief in his expression. "You think you know Spencer. Well, so do I. I know he's hiding something and I'm going to prove that it's murder." Her eyes locked with his. She wanted desperately for him to believe her, needed desperately for him to believe her, but saw that he couldn't because of the past he shared with Spencer

Donovan. "You and I don't have anything else to say to each other."

"Apparently not, since you seem to have your mind made up no matter what."

She turned and walked to her car, not looking back. He didn't follow her. When she reached her door, she turned. Bridger had gone to his pickup and stopped to look back at her. Their gazes met and held for an instant. Then he looked away as he climbed inside his truck, started the engine and pulled away.

As she opened her car door, she saw another yellow rose was lying on the driver's seat. Only this time there was no doubt in her mind that it was a warning. Or who had left it for her.

She shot a look toward the gravesite. Spencer stood alone on the hillside, his head bowed over Alyson's grave. His features were in shadow, but she knew he was watching her out of the corner of his eye. Watching her. And Bridger.

Chapter Eight

Laci went straight home and got on the Internet to see what she could find out about Spencer Donovan now that she knew Bridger and Spencer had grown up in Roundup, Montana. She had a place to start, at least.

As far as the sheriff and the authorities in Hawaii were concerned, the case was closed, but she couldn't let it go. Her instincts told her there was a lot more to the story.

As she worked, she tried not to think about Bridger. What did she know about the man, anyway? Hardly anything. He was still as much a mystery to her as he was to the rest of Old Town Whitehorse and the county.

So why did she feel that she knew him on an even more intimate level than lovemaking? She remembered cooking with him in his kitchen, that feeling of being home. Isn't that why his friendship with Spencer felt so much like a betrayal?

She could just imagine what her sister Laney would have to say about it. Laney would flip if she even knew that Laci had been hanging around with the Mystery Man of Old Town Whitehorse, let alone having been to bed with him.

Or possibly worse—that Laci had broken her promise and was now about to go after Spencer Donovan. She typed in *Roundup, Montana* and *Spencer Donovan*, then waited to see what came up on the screen. It felt good to be doing something about Alyson's death even if it turned out she was wrong about Spencer, wrong about Alyson's drowning being murder.

A high school alumni Web site came up on the screen, and her heart began to pound as she stared at the photos. Apparently Spencer had been one of the popular kids, so he showed up in a series of random shots.

There were photos of a younger Spencer in both basketball and football uniforms. His motto, according to the caption under one of his photos, was Take No Prisoners.

But it was a photograph with one of his teammates that caught her attention. Spencer and a boy named Tom Simpson had apparently been close friends. The two were photographed together, Spencer's arm resting on Tom's shoulders, both of them grinning at the camera.

It didn't take her long to find Tom Simpson. Tom had become an attorney and still lived and worked in Roundup.

Laci copied down the information, grabbed her purse and headed for the door. She could be in Roundup in less than two hours. Too bad Montana had done away with its no-speed-limit law, otherwise she could be there even sooner.

BRIDGER WAS STOCKING the pantry at the restaurant, cursing himself because he couldn't get Laci Cavanaugh out of his mind and yet knowing the best thing he could do was get as far away from that woman as possible, when he looked up and saw his sister, Eve Bailey, standing in the doorway.

It was the expression on her face that stopped him cold. He quickly climbed down and ushered her to a chair.

"What's wrong?" he asked, still surprised how easily he could read her——but, then again, they had shared the same womb and the same genes.

"They were razing what was left of Dr. Holloway's office building and the construction crew found something," Eve said. "A steel box. The sheriff has taken it to his office and is trying to find someone who can open it. The lid got too hot in the fire. It's going to take a welding torch to open it. They aren't even sure the contents will still be intact." She stopped, tears in her eyes. "But this could be what we've been looking for."

He'd thought this moment would complete him. He was finally going to know the truth. He should have been ecstatic, but instead all he felt was anxious and strangely afraid.

He reached for Eve's hand and squeezed it, seeing that she, too, was shaken. "You've been waiting for this for so long," he said. For him it had only been months and yet it seemed like a lifetime.

"I'm scared," his sister admitted, something he knew was hard for her. Eve had the exterior of a porcupine. She hated to show any vulnerability. They had that in common. "We may wish the truth had died with Doc."

"We have the right to know who our mother was and, if possible, the circumstances of our conception and birth."

Eve smiled ruefully. "Having the right is one thing, actually facing that knowledge…" She shook her head. "Isn't it enough to know we were adopted?"

"Maybe for you," he said, knowing she'd been as desperate as he was to know the truth. Had her desire cooled, as his had recently? "I want to know who she was, the circumstances, no matter what I learn." Was that true? He hoped to hell it was.

She nodded. "I told Carter to call us when he gets the box open. He's promised he will." She hesitated. "He's worried about what's inside, what it will do to you and me and the others, the Whitehorse Sewing Circle babies—the ones who don't know they were adopted."

She didn't have to add that the sheriff

would be most worried about what the contents would do to Eve. Bridger had seen the love in that man's eyes for Eve Bailey. According to local scuttlebutt, Carter Jackson had hurt Eve back in high school, dumped her for someone else who he'd married and later divorced. But Eve was having trouble forgiving him. It didn't help that Carter's ex had almost killed her.

He could understand her lack of forgiveness. He was still wrestling with that, angry at his adoptive parents even though both were now dead. It was hard to trust again.

That's why he knew he had to distance himself from Laci Cavanaugh. He reminded himself that his interest in her had originally only been to find out what she knew about her grandmother's underground adoption agency.

Right. So how did he explain that he'd never gotten around to asking Laci about the Whitehorse Sewing Circle?

Because he'd found out that she cooked and he'd gotten sidetracked.

He knew it was more than that. There was something about Laci Cavanaugh that was captivating. An innocence. A mule-headed stubbornness. An enthusiasm about life that was contagious.

He shook his head. The woman also saw killers where there were none. The only smart thing to do was to give her a wide berth and not give Laci Cavanaugh another thought.

If only he could.

"If the records are in that box, we'll need to decide what to do with them," Eve was saying. "We've kept the adoptions secret and our relationship secret—"

"We only did that because there was no evidence," Bridger said, angry that Laci had gotten back into his thoughts. "If that box does hold information about the babies, I wonder how many there will be." He and Eve knew they weren't the only babies adopted out by the sewing circle. In fact, Bridger suspected their adoptions were just the tip of the iceberg.

"Carter's afraid Glen Whitaker might hear about what was found at the site," Eve said. "You know he's been poking around ever since we found out the truth."

Bridger nodded. "I saw him out in Old Town this morning. Let's hope he's still out there. But you have to realize this isn't something we're going to be able to keep quiet if that box holds the adoption records. Don't we owe it to the others to let them know? And I know people are wondering about our relationship."

"I guess that's something we'll have to decide when the time comes. Don't you sometimes wish you'd never learned the truth?" she asked.

Part of him definitely did. This whole thing had thrown a monkey wrench into his life, leaving him feeling off-kilter, unsure about the future, unsure about himself. Except when he'd been with Laci.

"Sometimes I do," he admitted. "But then I would never have known I had a twin sister."

Eve smiled. "A sister you didn't want any part of, as I recall."

"I'm still sorry that was how I felt originally. I was angry and upset. I thought you were in on it."

She nodded. "All water under that particular bridge now, huh?" She glanced at her watch. "I'm going to go by the nursing home and see my grandmother while I wait for Carter's call. He promised not to open the box until we're there. I hope you're right about Glen Whitaker being down in Old Town. I'd hate to see this on the front page of the *Milk River Examiner.*"

But as she left, Bridger knew that the story coming out might be the least of their worries.

AFTER PHOTOGRAPHING Alice Miller's birthday party and eating too much cake and ice cream, Glen Whitaker got into his SUV outside the Whitehorse Community Center and checked to make sure he'd got enough photographs of the old lady and her friends.

He clicked on the digital photos, quickly reviewing what he'd taken at the party but more interested in the ones he'd gotten at the funeral.

He'd managed to get some of Spencer Donovan and Bridger Duvall standing together over the casket. Given the turnout, maybe his editor would deem it worthy of the front page.

Unfortunately, he hadn't been able to get an interview with Spencer Donovan. Glen had waited until almost everyone had left but Donovan. He'd gotten a few good photos of the man standing alone with the casket. And then he'd seen the mysterious brunette who was never far away when Donovan was around.

Glen had spotted her and even gotten several photographs before she'd seen him snapping her photo and taken off. Donovan had also seen the woman and had taken off right after that as though the hounds of hell had been after him.

And Glen had been left with the feeling that he finally had some bargaining power to get that interview. He dialed Spencer Donovan's cell.

"I told you I wasn't interested in—" Donovan started in the moment the reporter announced who was calling, but Glen cut him off.

"I know about the other woman," Glen said, bluffing, but he was rewarded with Donovan's sharp intake of breath. "We should talk."

"Do you know where the Banning ranch is?" Donovan asked.

"Of course." He checked his watch. He wanted to stop by Bridger Duvall's first. "I could be there in, say, an hour?"

"Fine. I'll see you then." Donovan hung up and Glen grinned to himself. So his suspicions about the brunette and Spencer Donovan had been on the money. He loved it when he was right.

So had Donovan hooked up with the brunette quickly after his wife's death? Or had the woman been there the whole time, waiting in the wings?

It certainly cast a new light on Alyson Banning Donovan's drowning in Hawaii.

As Glen drove down to the old McAllister place, there was no sign of Bridger Duvall's pickup. But then, he'd seen Duvall head toward Whitehorse after the funeral, no doubt back to his restaurant. It amazed Glen that the man didn't even have a dog to keep an eye on the place. He got out of his rig and walked toward the house.

Duvall's big black car was parked in the barn. The man at least had the good sense to buy a four-wheel-drive truck. It was required if you were going to live in this part of Montana and drive mostly unpaved roads.

He wondered if Duvall had already moved out of here. The place definitely had an unlived-in look about it, Glen thought as he peered in the windows before he tried the front door.

Unlocked. Which would make a man think Duvall had nothing to hide. Or, like a lot of these old places, the lock didn't work. He'd started to enter when he heard a vehicle coming up the road.

"Damn." He rushed to his rig, started it up and pulled around behind the barn just an instant before he saw a pickup top the rise.

Getting out, he edged to the corner of the building as the truck came to a stop in front of the house. He'd been betting it wasn't Bridger Duvall, and his instincts had proven him right.

Spencer Donovan climbed out of the pickup and glanced around as if looking for someone—and Glen swore to himself. Donovan had followed him!

At the front door of the house, Donovan

knocked, then stuck his head inside. He had to know that Bridger wasn't here. But then, Donovan wasn't looking for Bridger, was he?

Glen realized that this must have to do with the brunette. He glanced down at his camera hanging around his neck. Donovan must know that Glen had photographs of the woman.

Glancing around, Glen spotted a pile of hay stacked against the side of the barn. He took off the camera and stuffed it deep in the hay, then went back to his spot at the edge of the barn, not looking forward to a run-in with Donovan if it came to that since he was trespassing.

Glen didn't see Spencer Donovan and was wondering where he had gone when he heard a metal clang behind him. He was frowning, wondering what had made that sound, as he looked back toward his vehicle but saw nothing.

He turned to peer around the end of the barn again, looking toward the house, worried about where Donovan had gone. That's when he heard the soft scuff of a boot heel on dirt directly behind him.

Glen spun around and came face-to-face with the business end of a shovel. He didn't even have time to raise his arm to deflect the blow. The metal made a hollow clanging sound as it struck, the pain blinding as it ricocheted through his skull.

His knees buckled as the ground came rushing up at him, but before he reached it he heard the second blow of the shovel—not that he felt it.

Glen Whitaker was dead before he hit the ground.

LACI WAS JUST LEAVING her house when the pickup Spencer Donovan had been driving came roaring up in her yard.

Before she could retreat back into the house, he was out of the truck and stalking toward her.

"What are you doing here?" Laci demanded.

"I have to talk to you," he said. "Could I come in?"

"No." She clutched the edge of the door, ready to slam and lock it if he came any closer.

"I don't understand why you're acting as if you're afraid of me," he said from the porch, sounding hurt.

"I *know.*" It was out before she could call it back. "I saw the way you looked at Alyson at the reception."

Spencer stared at her. "What are you talking about?"

"You were on the dance floor. Alyson was visiting with one of the guests, and I saw your expression suddenly change." She saw the flicker of recognition in his eyes.

He stepped back, looked away, ran a hand over his face.

"I saw your face. I knew you were going to hurt her. I—"

"You're wrong," he said, raising his voice. "I thought I saw someone I used to—never mind. You think I killed my wife because of some look you thought I gave her? That's *crazy.*"

"That's what you want everyone to think. But Alyson is dead. And we both know she was a strong swimmer."

"A much stronger swimmer than me," Spencer said. "That's why I wasn't with her." He looked away. "The truth is…I'm afraid of water." His gaze came back to hers.

"How convenient." She started to close the door. "And stop leaving those stupid yellow roses in my car!"

He blanched and looked around as if afraid someone had heard her. "*What?*"

"You heard me. Just leave me alone and stop threatening me." She stepped back to close the door, but he moved fast for his size. He stuck his foot in between the door and the jamb and shoved the door open, knocking her back as he took a step toward her. A scream rose in her throat as he grabbed her wrist, his fingers digging into her flesh.

"Don't do this," he said, his voice breaking. "You really don't want to do this."

She jerked free, scrambling toward the kitchen and the phone, praying she could reach it before he caught her. She jerked up the phone and dialed 9-1-1. The line began to ring. She turned, expecting to find him standing before her, ready to stop her.

But the kitchen was empty.

"9-1-1 operator. How may I help you?" the dispatcher said on the other end of the line.

Laci couldn't speak—just as she hadn't been able to scream earlier. She stepped cautiously to the kitchen doorway. Her front door stood open. She moved toward it.

"9-1-1 operator. Please tell me your emergency."

She hadn't gone far when she saw Spencer. He was walking down her driveway to his truck. She rushed to the front door, closing, locking and leaning against it.

"Hello?" the dispatcher said, sounding worried.

"I'm sorry. It was a false alarm." Laci hung up, her heart a sledgehammer in her chest. Tears blurred her eyes. She couldn't remember ever being so frightened.

She moved to the window, afraid Spencer was still out there, but his truck was pulling away.

She was right about him. Was it possible he would turn himself in now? She could only hope.

But in the back of her mind she kept asking herself: if Spencer Donovan was a killer, then why hadn't he come after her in the kitchen? Or was he just biding his time? Waiting for an opportunity to make it look like an accident, the same why he had Alyson's death?

All she knew was that she had to find evidence against him to get the case reopened—before she was next.

ATTORNEY TOM SIMPSON had an office uptown in a two-story brick building in Roundup, Montana, that said he wasn't as successful as he would have liked.

Laci hadn't called ahead, having a feeling that Tom wasn't going to want to talk to her. There was no secretary behind the front desk. Still at lunch, although it was almost two? Or on an errand?

Through his open door she saw him sitting behind his desk. He'd taken off his suit jacket. It hung on the back of his chair. She noted the gold wedding band on his left hand and a photograph of a woman and two small children on the corner of his desk.

He had his feet propped up on the old radiator by the window and was eating what looked like a turkey-and-cheese sandwich on white that his wife must have made him that morning for lunch but that he hadn't got around to eating until now. He was eating and gazing out the window, and for a moment Laci regretted that she had to disturb him.

"Mr. Simpson?"

Startled, he swung around and put down his sandwich as he reached for his suit jacket to cover up the mayo stain on his white shirt.

"Please don't let me interrupt your late lunch," she said, taking a chair across from his desk.

"I'm sorry—did we have an appointment?" he asked, glancing at his watch. "My secretary is out."

She shook her head and took a chair across from his desk. "I just stopped by to talk to you about Spencer Donovan."

Tom frowned. "Who?"

"Oh, you must remember Spencer Donovan." She'd photocopied several of the pages from the Internet class reunion site and now passed him the one of the two young teammates grinning at the camera.

He took the sheet of paper reluctantly,

barely glancing at it before handing the photo back. "Actually, right now isn't—"

"I'll be quick," Laci said, giving him her best smile. "Of course, your comments will be kept confidential."

"What is this about?"

"Spencer recently married my best friend. She drowned while swimming on their honeymoon." She refused to call it an accident and had to bite her tongue not to tell Tom that she knew Spencer had killed Alyson. But she feared he would take her for a nutcase and call the cops to throw her out if she didn't go at this carefully.

After her run-in with Spencer, Laci was more determined than ever to find evidence that would get Alyson's case reopened. She felt as if Spencer were a ticking time bomb. She had to act quickly—before her time ran out.

Tom Simpson looked sick to hear the news about the honeymoon death. "Poor Spencer."

Yes, poor Spencer. "I'd like to help Spencer through this but I don't know him very well. You knew him. Tell me about him."

"Well, it was years ago—"

"That's what I'm interested in. What was he like in high school?" she said, drawing her chair closer to his desk. "I just get the impression this isn't the first tragedy he's had in his life."

Tom looked sick. He picked up his sandwich, dropped it into the container it had been packaged in and shoved it into a desk drawer. She gave him time, knowing he was making up his mind about talking to her. Did that mean there was something to tell?

"I don't know what to say. He suffered some football injuries." He shrugged. "Other than that…"

She saw the change in his expression as he remembered something. "What?"

"Well, there was this girl in high school…."

Of course there was, Laci thought. "Don't tell me. She died, right?"

BRIDGER COULDN'T concentrate on work. He kept thinking about the box that had been found in the ruins of Dr. Holloway's office and what might be inside it.

And he couldn't help worrying about Laci. He'd hoped that telling her about Spencer saving his life would make her understand not only why he owed the man but also why Spencer couldn't have killed anyone.

But as short a time as he'd known Laci, he knew she wouldn't rest until she— Until she what?

He felt a jolt. Until she found out everything there was to know about Spencer Donovan. So why did that scare him so much?

His heart was pounding as he picked up the phone and called her home number, praying she would be home and not off investigating Spencer. No answer. He didn't leave a message.

He tried her cell. A message came up on the screen. Caller out of area? He swore as he hung up. Where had she gone? Who was he kidding? She'd gone to Roundup. She'd find out everything about Spencer.

But there was nothing to find. Laci would eventually realize she was wrong. She *was* wrong, wasn't she? He didn't believe for a minute that Spencer could kill anyone, right?

As if he'd conjured him up, the back door of the restaurant opened and Spencer walked in.

"The place is looking great," Spencer said, glancing around the kitchen before stepping into the dining room.

All the tables had come, as well as the chairs. The building was starting to look like a real restaurant.

There was art on the walls and tablecloths and candles on each table. With luck, the restaurant would be open before Christmas.

But Spencer barely gave the place a look. He appeared nervous as he glanced around the kitchen. "So where is your junior chef?" he asked, the question leaving little doubt he'd come here looking for Laci.

"Working up some menu ideas for me," Bridger said, wondering why when it came to Laci he lied to Spencer.

"Really? I thought I saw her heading down the highway out of town earlier."

Bridger felt his heart lodge in his throat. He'd forgotten that Spencer was staying at the old Banning place just down the road from Laci's. He had no idea where she was at this very moment, but he'd wager it was somewhere on the road to trouble.

"Did you need her for something?" Bridger asked, a little unnerved by Spencer's interest in Laci.

He seemed to hesitate. "I would imagine you know that she thinks I had something to do with Alyson's death."

Bridger winced. He'd known this was going to happen. "She's just upset."

"I don't think so. Someone had been in my house while I was gone. They'd gone through my belongings."

"Laci wouldn't…." Bridger let the words die off. In the state she was in, maybe she would. "I'll talk to her."

"Thanks, but I'm not sure that will do any good."

He studied Spencer, seeing a state of anxiety that worried him. "Something else?"

Spencer looked uncomfortable. "That reporter—Glen Whitaker? He called me earlier. He's been trying to get an interview. I finally gave up and decided to talk to him, but he never showed."

"That's odd." Bridger couldn't help but

wonder why Spencer had agreed to talk to the man.

"I would imagine he's just doing the same thing Laci Cavanaugh is—digging for dirt. I really wish she wouldn't do that."

Bridger didn't know what to say.

"Sometimes I feel as if I'm losing my mind. I keep seeing her…." Spencer shook his head as if shaking off the horrific memory.

"It was an accident. You can't blame yourself. Alyson wouldn't want that."

Spencer nodded after a moment. "I froze. I stood there on the beach. Just the thought of going into the water…"

Bridger felt that old familiar anvil of guilt on his chest. He was responsible for Spencer's fear of water. And because of that, wasn't he at least partially responsible for Alyson's death, as well?

"Spencer, if you hadn't jumped into that creek that day to save me…"

"I didn't bring it up to make you feel bad. It's just that you're the only person who can understand why I hesitated to save my own wife. It just brought it all back—the nightmares, everything from the past." Spencer rubbed a trembling hand over his face. "I'm not sure how much more I can take, you know?"

Bridger shifted uncomfortably on his feet. He didn't know what to say, let alone what to do.

Spencer seemed to pull himself together after a moment. "I've decided to leave town. I think as long as I'm around, it will only make things worse. I've put the ranch up for sale. Before you hear it from someone else, I've also sold the drilling rights to a gas and oil company. Apparently the land is worth more than Alyson and I thought."

Motive. Bridger swore to himself. Spencer had just provided a motive for murdering his wife. He tried to hide his surprise—and worry that Spencer might have known about the gas and oil *before* he married Alyson.

"I can't stay here with Alyson's best friend thinking I'm a monster," Bridger was saying. "I wish you could get her to stop this."

Yeah, Bridger thought, so did he. As if he

hadn't already tried that. "What does it matter what she thinks? With you leaving, you'll probably never see her again." At least he hoped to hell that would be the case.

Spencer shook his head. "Still, it hurts me to think that Alyson's best friend hates me. I know it shouldn't be messing with my head the way it is, but I don't think I can live with her believing I'm a murderer."

Chapter Nine

The steel box sat on Sheriff Carter Jackson's desk, unopened, when Bridger arrived only moments after the call. Bridger had said goodbye to Spencer, unable to hide his relief that the man was leaving town.

Eve Bailey stopped pacing, her eyes locking with Bridger's as he stepped in and closed the door. It was the moment they'd both been waiting for. If they were right, the name of at least their mother and possibly the circumstances of their adoptions were in that box.

The sheriff lifted the lid and stepped back.

Just as Bridger had hoped, the box was filled with file folders, yellowed with age. He reached in and drew one out, handing it to Eve, before he took one for himself, his hand shaking as he opened it.

"It's the babies," Eve cried.

He barely heard her over the thunder of his pulse.

Eve sat down as if her legs would no longer hold her up.

Bridger's hands were shaking as he scanned the contents of the file in his hand and frowned. He picked up another and did the same before he swore.

"It's not here," he said as he flipped through more files.

"*What?*" he heard Eve say behind him. "*No.*" She was on her feet, scanning the file in her hand. She threw it down on the desk and looked over at Bridger, tears in her eyes.

"What is it?" Carter asked, stepping closer. "Aren't they the adoption files?"

"Oh, they're the files, all right," Bridger said. "The answers are even here. There's just one problem—there are no names, no dates, nothing to know which of these files is ours."

"That's not possible," Carter said, picking up the file Eve had dropped.

Bridger studied the one in his hand. "These are worthless without the key to the code."

"Code?" Carter asked.

"At the bottom of every record," Bridger said.

Eve pulled out a file, read it and let out a curse. "You can't be serious. Animals and colors?"

"And flowers," Carter said from the sidelines. "I see what you mean."

Each file had the name of an animal, a color or a flower neatly printed at the bottom. Leave it to a bunch of old ladies to come up with *this!*

"So we don't know any more than we did," Eve said.

Bridger grasped a ray of hope. "We *will* know, though, once we have the key to the code."

"But I thought this would end it. I thought we'd finally know and it would be over, that we could quit wondering and searching," Eve said, sounding close to bawling. Carter stepped to her, wrapping her in his arms.

"It's more than we had, Eve. We're in here somewhere," Bridger said, holding up a handful of the files. "We should be relieved that Dr. Holloway kept any records at all."

She nodded, clearly fighting tears, and burrowed her face into the sheriff's chest. Suddenly the office seemed too small, too intimate. Bridger put the files back into the box.

"You'll put these away somewhere safe until we can find the codes?" he asked Carter.

The sheriff nodded. "Don't worry. I'll take care of it."

Bridger glanced at Eve still in the sheriff's arms.

"I'll take care of that, too," Carter said.

Bridger nodded and smiled, happy that Eve and Carter had each other. He'd spent so much of his life alone and thought he was completely content with his own company. Until Laci. Now he felt empty without her. Did any of this matter anymore? He'd thought finding out the truth about his birth would fill that emptiness, but it had been Laci who'd filled it.

Once outside the sheriff's department, he dialed Laci's cell phone number again. It rang four times before her voice mail picked up.

"Hey," he said, trying to hide his disappointment and instantly at a loss as to what to say. "I was just thinking about you." So true. "Call me, okay?"

He felt like a fool as he hung up. What was he going to say when she called him back? *I miss you?* It was true. Or maybe he'd say *I'm worried about you.* Also true.

But what about what Spencer had told him? Had Laci gone into Spencer's house, gone through his things? Bridger didn't want to believe it. But he'd seen how determined she was. He hated to think of her reaction when she heard about the money Spencer would make off the Banning ranch.

The more he thought about it, the more anxious he became. Spencer had been acting so oddly at the restaurant earlier. Acting… afraid. Afraid of what Laci would find out about him? Or what the reporter already knew?

Snapping off his phone, Bridger walked to his pickup, hoping Laci called back soon. Better yet, that she'd get back here. Was there any chance Spencer knew where Laci had gone—and had possibly gone after her?

Spencer had been acting like a man with his back to the wall earlier. A *guilty* man.

Which would make Laci right. And make Spencer Donovan a dangerous man.

LACI TOOK A BREATH as she stared across the desk at Tom Simpson. "Tell me about the girl."

"There isn't much to tell, really," Tom said. "It was our senior year in high school. Spencer was dating a freshman named Emma Shane. He broke up with her. It was high school—you know how that goes. But Emma flipped out. She tried to kill him by attacking him with a knife at school. Failing that, she ran home and set her house on fire, killing herself and her parents."

Laci shuddered. "No one was able to save her or her family?"

"There was a large propane tank next to the house, but by the time the firemen arrived… The tank blew, completely incinerating the house and everyone inside."

"Was there any chance Spencer set the fire?"

Tom recoiled in shock at the question.

"No, of course not. Spencer was with me. When the fire broke out, we were at football practice. We went over to see what was going on when we heard the sirens. Why would you ask that?"

She changed the subject. "Were you friends with Bridger Duvall, as well?"

"Not really. Bridger was two years younger. He didn't play football. He rodeoed. He and Spencer were neighbors but didn't hang out together in high school. If you know about Bridger, then you probably know that Spencer saved his life when they were kids. Made the front page of the paper. Spencer was a hero in Roundup."

She didn't know what to say. She'd thought the moment she heard about the girl's death she would have found *something* incriminating in Spencer's past.

"Emma had some mental problems," Tom was saying. "No one blamed Spencer for what happened, but I think he blamed himself. He wasn't the same after that. He went away to college. His family moved. As far as I know, he never came back to Roundup."

"End of story," she said more to herself than him.

"I'm afraid that's all I can tell you."

Another death. But Spencer Donovan apparently had nothing to do with it. Except for breaking up with the girl, who apparently had been unstable.

Just an unfortunate accident. Like Alyson's drowning.

"You two didn't keep in touch during college, then?" she asked, thinking maybe it wasn't all that strange. She'd lost track of people she'd known from high school—just not her close friends.

"Spencer went to Montana State University in Bozeman," Tom said. "I went to school in Arizona. Our lives took different paths."

"Do you know of anyone else who might have kept in touch with him?" she asked.

Tom shook his head. "Wasn't there anyone from here at the wedding?"

"No," she said, frowning. As far as she knew, Bridger had been the only person there on the groom's side. "Not even his family was there."

Tom shrugged. "His parents are probably gone by now. He was an only child, and both of his parents were older than the rest of ours."

She couldn't believe she'd hit another dead end. "Thank you," she said, getting to her feet and seeing his relief. "I'll tell Spencer hello for you."

"That's not necessary. I mean, he probably wouldn't even remember me."

She heard something in Tom's voice. He hadn't just lost track of Spencer, he'd let the friendship go. Was there a reason? Something that had happened other than the girl's death? Clearly Tom wasn't interested in having Spencer Donovan back in his life.

But as he retrieved his sandwich and took a bite, she knew whatever the reason, Tom Simpson wasn't going to tell her.

On her way out Laci noticed that his secretary, an elderly gray-haired woman, had returned and was sitting at her desk. She seemed about to say something to Laci when Tom called her into his office. She hurried in and closed the door.

Outside the building, Laci checked her

cell phone and saw that Bridger had called several times. She listened to his messages, hearing in his voice how worried he was about her.

Who could blame him since it seemed she was trying to condemn a man for murder who'd had his share of bad luck already. A man who had nothing to hide.

"Hi," she said when Bridger answered. She knew she must sound a little contrite. And for a good reason.

"Hi." He sounded relieved to hear her voice. "You all right?"

"Yeah."

"I was hoping you might want to have some dinner with me tonight."

She glanced at her watch. "It would have to be late. I'm in Roundup."

"I figured. Everything okay?"

No. She felt hot tears burn her eyes. She'd been so sure about Spencer. Everyone had tried to tell her she was wrong about him, but she'd refused to believe it.

"I've been better," she admitted, realizing she might have been on this quest to convict

Spencer of murder so she didn't have to deal with her grief over Alyson's death.

"Then a nice dinner might help?"

"Yes, it might," she said, smiling into the phone.

"Good. Just come by the restaurant when you get back to Whitehorse."

"Thank you. For everything," she added, feeling guilty and full of gratitude that he was being so nice after she'd been so awful about Spencer. "I'll see you soon."

"Laci? Be careful."

"I always drive carefully."

It wasn't until she hung up that she realized he might not be talking about her driving. She couldn't wait to see him, she realized as she dropped her phone back into her purse.

Now maybe she could put all this foolishness about Spencer behind her. Alyson was dead. She'd drowned in a swimming accident. Laci couldn't bring her back. She just had to accept that her best friend was gone. And no one was to blame for her death.

Wiping at her tears, Laci dug out her keys to open her car when she heard a door swing wide behind her.

"Miss?"

Laci turned to see Tom's elderly secretary motion to her. Curious, Laci stepped back toward the building.

"I overheard you asking about Spencer Donovan," the woman said conspiratorially. "I knew his mother. Bless her soul." She looked behind her as if afraid her boss might have seen her come out of the building. "You should talk to Patty. She owns the Mint Bar downtown." The woman looked as if she wanted to say more but suddenly clamped her lips shut. "Just talk to Patty," she said and, turning around, disappeared back into the building.

BRIDGER TOOK A FEW moments to enjoy his relief before he started planning what to make Laci for dinner. She'd sounded good on the phone. Obviously she hadn't found out anything incriminating about Spencer. Maybe now she could start healing.

He planned what to cook, only a little surprised how excited he was about seeing her again. All his attempts to exorcise her from his thoughts had failed miserably. He'd only been kidding himself that he wouldn't see her again.

Mentally he made his list on the way to the market.

But as he started back toward the restaurant, telling himself not to worry about Laci, he thought of the files he and Eve had seen earlier. They'd come so close to learning the truth about their birth.

Impulsively he turned the pickup around and headed out to the nursing home as he recalled his last visit and the woman who'd stopped by Pearl's room—Bertie Cavanaugh. He hadn't had a chance to speak to the woman. But he had plenty of time now, he thought as he checked to make sure Titus wasn't here visiting before he swung into the parking lot.

Bertie Cavanaugh was a large-boned, gray-haired woman with a perpetual scowl. She turned that scowl on him as he tapped at her open door.

Eyes narrowing, she demanded, "What do you want?"

"I'm Bridger Duvall," he said, although from her tone he suspected she already knew that. He stepped into her room, leaving the door open.

She sat on the end of her bed, a doll in her lap. When he'd first looked into her room, she'd been whispering something to the doll as she'd brushed its hair.

He knew this was probably a waste of time, but he had nothing to lose at this point. "How are you today?"

"Same as I always am," she snapped.

He tried a different tack. "What is your doll's name?"

She looked down at the toy in her lap and seemed surprised to see it. "Baby," she said with a soft, almost loving tone.

"She's pretty," he said, sitting down in the chair near the bed.

Bertie lifted her gaze to his, suspicion in her eyes again. "What do you want?"

"I want to know about the Whitehorse Sewing Circle," he said, sensing that there was nothing wrong with Bertie Cavanaugh's mind. "Were you a member?"

"For almost fifty years." There was pride in her voice as her chin came up.

"That's a long time," he said, trying to

hide his excitement. Bertie would have been a member when he was brought to the old Whitehorse Cemetery to be adopted. But he worried that not all of the members might have known about the adoptions given how long the secret had been kept.

"Whose idea was it to use colors and flowers and animals as codes on the files?"

"Pearl's," she said without hesitation.

His heart was pounding so hard he thought it might burst. For the second time today he felt so close to learning the truth he could almost taste it.

"Who kept track of which symbol went with each baby?" he asked and held his breath.

Bertie studied him. "You're one of them, aren't you?" she finally said.

He nodded. "Thirty-two years ago my parents picked me up from a woman in the Whitehorse Cemetery."

Bertie nodded. "I recall hearing about that." She began to brush the doll's hair again.

"I need to know who my mother was."

"You know who your mother was," she

said without looking up. "The one who took care of you."

"My *birth* mother."

Bertie let out an annoyed sound. "I'm tired. You should go. I have to get Baby's hair done before dinner."

"Bertie—"

"Leave," she snapped and met his gaze. "Leave before I call the nurse and tell her you were bothering me."

He rose from the chair. "I'm sorry I bothered you."

"Me, too," she said and went back to fixing Baby's hair.

As Bridger came out of the nursing home, he spotted Spencer standing beside his pickup, obviously waiting for him, and felt his stomach roil. This couldn't be good. He'd thought Spencer had left town.

"Visiting the old folks, huh?" Spencer asked, sounding amused. "You really are something," he said with a shake of his head.

Whatever Bridger was, it didn't sound like a compliment, and he realized that Spencer had been drinking. Great. As if things couldn't get any worse.

But at least Spencer hadn't followed Laci to Roundup.

"I just wanted to let you know I'm sorry."

"Sorry?"

Spencer wagged his head, looking close to tears. "You have no idea what I've been through. No idea."

Bridger couldn't argue that and didn't try. He could see that Spencer was even drunker than he'd originally thought.

"I just had to tell you that I'm sorry before I left. I won't be back."

Bridger tried not to let his relief show. "I'm sorry things didn't work out for you here."

"Sure you are," Spencer said sarcastically. "But they're working out for you. Things always work out for you, don't they, Bridger?"

He was surprised by the animosity he heard in Spencer's voice. "You aren't leaving tonight, I hope."

"Why, you worried I might kill myself on the highway?" Spencer's laugh was bitter. "That might be the best thing that could happen to me."

This kind of self-pity always put Bridger off. "Well, I wish you the best of luck."

"I'll need more than luck," Spencer said, sounding as despondent as he looked.

"You take care," he said as Spencer turned and disappeared into the shadows. A moment later the engine on his pickup engine fired up and Spencer left the lot in a hail of gravel.

"He's going to kill someone." Bridger reached for his cell, hating what he was about to do. But it was the best thing for Spencer—and whoever else was on the road tonight, including Laci. Maybe a night in jail would be the best thing for Spencer.

Or maybe it would turn out to be the worst thing Bridger had ever done to the man who'd saved his life. But he had a feeling he'd already done the worst thing he could do. He hadn't helped Spencer. Instead he'd fallen for a woman who was bound and determined to see Spencer behind bars for more than a night.

"SO YOU WANT THE GOODS on Spencer Donovan?" The woman's eyes shone with malicious humor. And alcohol.

Patty Waring had dark, straight hair cut chin-length, almond-shaped brown eyes and two empty shot glasses in front of her when Laci arrived at the bar.

"I was afraid you were going to miss happy hour," Patty said as she motioned to the cocktail waitress. "What are you having?"

"A diet cola," Laci told the waitress, who slid another shot in front of Patty.

"Killjoy," Patty said with good humor and patted the circular booth seat next to her. "So what is it you're looking for? And why?"

Laci liked the woman's straightforward attitude and decided her best approach was some of the same. "Spencer Donovan married my best friend—and she died on their honeymoon."

Patty leaned back, eyes widening, and let out a "Well, hell." She picked up the shot glass and drained it without blinking an eye.

"It seems he's had bad luck in his relationships with women."

Patty laughed. "That's one way of putting it. I assume Tom told you about Emma."

Laci nodded. "Everyone thinks he's innocent, including the police. The same with this girl Emma. Spencer had an alibi. But I can't help but believe there's more, something in his past, some indication of the kind of man he really is."

"Anyone mention what happened at college?" Patty asked.

Laci shook her head, knowing what was coming. Her heart began to pound in her ears, all her old fears rising like the tide. "What happened?"

"More bad luck. One girl he was dating fell down the stairs in her dorm. She swore she was pushed. Another got trapped in the laundry room with a spilled bottle of ammonia."

"Spencer's doing?"

"Apparently the girls thought so. But Spencer had an alibi each time. There was a rumor that the girls had broken it off with him and he'd been furious." Patty shrugged. "You've got to understand, I never liked Spencer. He was stuck-up in high school— you know, the real jock type. He acted like he didn't know me at college. So I only heard stories about him. Who can say if they were true or not?"

"Like about the girls at the dorm?"

She nodded. "The fiancée was a whole different thing, though. It was in the newspapers."

"Fiancée?" Laci couldn't hide her surprise.

"You didn't know he was engaged to be married?" She let out a little laugh and motioned for another shot. "Tiffany Palmer. Pretty, rich, naïve. Spencer only dated girls with money."

"What happened to her?" Laci asked, her heart pounding.

"In a nutshell? Hit-and-run driver. Killed on impact. Never caught the guy." She smiled. "The kicker? The description of the car matched Spencer's. However," she added quickly, "Spencer had reported it stolen two days before the hit-and-run. Rumor—that sweet little Tiff had been having second thoughts about marrying him. Seems she wasn't wearing her engagement ring when she was killed." Patty sat back and shrugged.

"But Spencer was cleared again?"

Patty nodded. "Airtight alibi for the time of the hit-and-run."

The waitress set another shot in front of Patty, but she didn't reach for it.

Laci let out the breath she'd been holding. "He could have hidden his car for those two days before the hit-and-run," she said, thinking out loud. "He could have set up the whole thing. Got someone to lie for him." She saw Patty's expression. "You don't think he killed her. Why?"

"Personally? I don't think Spencer has it in him. Plus, he had an alibi."

"He always has an alibi," Laci said. Still no proof. But another woman dead. How many bodies would it take before someone realized that this man was either walking bad luck or a killer?

"That wasn't the end of it, though," Patty said as she picked up the shot glass and turned it slowly in her fingers. Her nails were long and painted bright red with tiny little martini glasses on each tip.

"The fiancée's cousin also attended MSU. Christy wasn't like her cuz. She lived on my floor, and we became friends when she heard I was also from Roundup. Christy was convinced that Spencer had been after her cousin's money and had killed Tiff. Christy was determined to prove it. She started asking a lot of questions on her own."

Laci realized she hadn't touched her diet cola and took a sip.

"Spencer got wind of it."

"He threatened her?"

Patty laughed. "He was too smart for that. One night Christy came back to the dorm and she was freaking. Seemed every time she turned around, Spencer was there."

Laci felt a jolt. Just as Spencer had been turning up a lot around her.

"Then he started leaving her little souvenirs, and she just couldn't take it anymore. She went to the cops, afraid for her life, but of course she couldn't prove that Spencer had done anything, including stalking her. She quit school and that was the last I heard of her."

Laci's heart hammered. "*Souvenirs?*"

"Get this—a single yellow rose."

Chapter Ten

Not for the first time, Sheriff Carter Jackson got a call from the owner of the *Milk River Examiner* reporting that Glen Whitaker was missing.

It came on the heels of a call from Bridger Duvall about his friend Spencer Donovan. Carter had one of his deputies pick up Donovan. He'd just hung up when Mark Sanders called.

The problem with being a sheriff in a small town was that more people knew his home number than his office number.

"I hate to bother you at home," Sanders said in an excited, worried voice. "But Glen went out to Old Town to do a story on Alice Miller's ninetieth birthday party and hasn't been seen since. He knew I needed those photographs for tomorrow's paper. This isn't like him."

The sheriff remembered another time Glen had gone missing. That time he'd turned up beside a county road, beaten, his vehicle crashed in a ditch and with no memory of what had happened.

"You're sure he doesn't hit the bottle on occasion and this isn't like last time?" he asked.

"Absolutely not," Sanders said. "Glen doesn't touch the stuff. Something has to have happened to him."

The sheriff groaned to himself. "I'll send a deputy out to look for him. Was he planning to do anything else besides cover Alice's birthday party?"

"Not that I know of," Sanders said. "He's been trying to get an interview with Spencer Donovan...."

Great. "Okay, I'll do some checking and get back to you. You'll call if you hear from him?"

"I really need the photographs in his camera," Sanders said.

"I'll tell the deputy to be on the lookout for his camera," Carter said and hung up. He got on the radio and asked one of the deputies to drive down to Old Town White-horse and see what he could find out. He hoped Charlotte Evans wasn't up to her old tricks of taking out her frustrations on un-suspecting men.

Glen, he figured, would turn up. He did last time. Eventually.

IN A FOG OF ANGER and grief, Laci got into her car to drive home. Grief for the sense-less death of her friend. Anger not only that Spencer was a killer, just as she'd suspected, but that she might never be able to prove it.

Even if she could prove he'd left her the roses, it didn't make him a killer. And proving stalking in Whitehorse would be im-possible. The town was too small—of course they would run across each other.

She was so upset that at first she didn't notice. But as she started her car, she sensed she was being watched.

There were a half dozen cars parked on the street. She didn't see anyone. But she couldn't shake the feeling that she wasn't alone. Spencer? Was it possible he'd followed her to Roundup? Or was it merely her overactive imagination in full swing?

As she pulled out, she glanced in her rearview mirror but didn't see anyone following her.

Unnerved and anxious to get back to Whitehorse—and Bridger—she drove faster than she probably should have. She knew her fears were justified. Was it just a matter of time before Spencer stopping threatening her with roses and set her up for an "accident"?

She was in such a state that she didn't even remember driving the hours to Whitehorse.

As she pulled up in front of the restaurant, she saw that there was a light on inside. She could see a shadow moving around in the back. Bridger. He was waiting for her with a nice dinner. He'd probably been cooking ever since they'd talked.

Her first impulse was to rush in there and tell him how wrong he was about Spencer Donovan. But in her heart she knew this wasn't Bridger's fault. Bridger hadn't known Spencer since they were kids. It wasn't fair to blame him. She could understand how he felt indebted to Spencer. After all, the boy next door had saved his life.

But she knew that wasn't why she couldn't spoil this evening. She needed Bridger to hold her, to make her feel safe, if even for a little while.

She couldn't go in there and tell him about Spencer. Not at first, anyway. What did she really have on Spencer? Nothing. Just like the cousin—Christy. The police in Roundup hadn't taken a single yellow rose as a threat any more than Sheriff Jackson would here in Whitehorse.

Laci sat for a moment, trying to pull herself together. *Don't spoil tonight.* She couldn't bear the thought Spencer would always be between them.

She saw Bridger come toward the front of the building. He must have heard her drive up, seen her headlights.

Just the sight of him warmed her to her toes. She thought of being inside his restaurant, thrilled to be with him. She cut the car's engine and climbed out.

He opened the front door of the restaurant,

his smile so broad there was no doubt that he'd missed her. Maybe even as much as she had him. He looked so handsome standing there. She felt a wave of desire as she stepped into his arms.

He held her close. "I've missed you," he breathed against her hair.

"Me, too." They stood like that for a long moment, holding each other, then moved apart, both seeming a little awkward, a little shy.

"I hope you're hungry," he said.

"Starved." For food, for him.

He ushered her inside. She took a deep breath, taking in the wonderful scents of the food, of the man next to her, and thought she could die at that moment and regret nothing.

"I made something special," Bridger was saying as he smiled and took her hand.

She let him lead her into the kitchen. He'd set a table at the back, complete with candles. She felt a wave of sentiment for this man. Not love. It couldn't be love, not this quickly, could it?

She felt a little guilty as she sat down, saw all the work he'd gone to, but mostly she realized that he believed she hadn't found out anything in Roundup, that she was through trying to prove Spencer Donovan was a killer.

She could see his relief and couldn't bear telling him differently. At least not yet.

LACI HADN'T SAID anything about her trip. That worried Bridger. But he wasn't about to ask. He didn't tell her that he'd called the sheriff about Spencer or that he was half-ashamed for doing it.

The last person he wanted to talk about was Spencer.

But he did need to talk to her. He studied her face in the flickering candlelight, feeling a pull stronger than gravity. There would be nothing standing in their way soon. Spencer would leave town and no longer be between them. He felt a twinge of guilt—not for having Spencer picked up and thrown in jail for the night but for wanting him out of their lives.

"You're amazing," Bridger said to Laci.

She smiled at him as she pushed back her plate. "Amazing?" She shook her head. "I'm stuffed, though. It was wonderful."

He grinned, pleased. "I'm glad you liked it."

"I loved it. I've never met anyone who understood the importance of cooking."

He held his breath as his eyes locked with hers. He'd promised himself they wouldn't fall right back into bed.

"Come on," he said. "I don't believe you've ever seen my rooftop."

"Rooftop?"

He took her hand and led her out back and up a flight of stairs to the roof.

"What do you think?" he asked as he walked her to the front edge. "From here you can see the northern lights on a clear night."

"It's breathtaking." She hugged herself against the cold night air, wondering why he'd brought her up here. "It scares me a little," she said, not realizing she'd spoken her fear out loud.

"Are you afraid of heights?" he asked, sounding alarmed.

"No, this thing between us. It's happened so fast...."

"You're afraid it isn't real."

She nodded.

"There is one way to tell."

She looked over at him, eager to hear it.

"One foolproof test that's infallible." He leaned toward her. "This."

His kiss was sweeter than the richest confection. She tasted him, reveling in the feel of his lips, the teasing of his tongue, the warmth of being wrapped in his arms.

His mouth sparked a desire in her that curled her toes. She felt fifteen again and knew just how dangerous that could be. Her lips parted and she drank him in. A sweet, deadly elixir. She felt intoxicated, drunk on this feeling and this man.

That alone should have warned her.

"Are we clear now?" he asked, drawing back to hold her gaze hostage.

"Perfectly clear," she said as he pulled her down for another kiss. She really had to get the recipe for this.

Bridger slipped his arm around her and pulled her closer. She raised her face to his kiss, her arms coming around his neck as her body pressed into his.

He held her, his mouth taking hers. She tasted faintly of vanilla.

For the last year since his mother had died

he'd been searching for who he was. But holding Laci, he knew what he'd needed and wanted. He felt as if he'd found it. Nothing mattered but getting to know this woman. They'd skipped some of the steps. Like her, he felt they were moving too fast. It scared him, as well, because they didn't know each other.

At least Laci didn't know him.

He drew back to look at her. "Laci, there's something I need to tell you. Why I came to Whitehorse. Why I've stayed."

He told her everything, from what his mother had confessed on her deathbed to his visits to the nursing home to why he'd originally decided to open the restaurant.

Laci frowned. "You planned our meeting the first time."

He nodded but quickly added, "I never even got around to asking you what you knew about the Whitehorse Sewing Circle. Once I met you…"

"No one else knows about this?" she asked.

"I asked your grandfather Titus about it

but he swears he knows nothing about it. I believe him. I had to tell you."

"So Eve is your twin sister?"

He nodded. "Some files were found, but unfortunately they're coded. Until we have the code…"

"And you're sure my grandmother is behind these adoptions?" she asked.

"I can't prove it until your grandmother regains her ability to speak."

She stepped away from him, hugging herself against the cold.

"We should go back inside," he said. "I didn't mean to just drop this on you, but I wanted you to know. I just thought you might like the view, and downstairs was a little too intimate. I needed a clear head. I was afraid of how you'd take the news."

She didn't turn to look at him. "Aren't you going to ask me if I know anything about the adoptions?"

"I don't need to. I know you would tell me if you knew anything." He placed his hand on her shoulder.

She turned, shrugging his hand off. "I'm sorry but I need to go home now."

"Laci—"

"I'm tired. A lot has happened. Thank you for a wonderful dinner, but I need to be alone."

"I've upset you. I'm sorry, but I had to be honest with you."

Laci nodded. "And I need to be honest with you." She told him everything she'd learned about Spencer Donovan, including about the yellow roses.

But as she finished she saw that he hadn't taken the threat seriously.

"They're *roses*."

"With *thorns*."

"Has he threatened to hurt you?"

"No. But don't you see? The man is dangerous. Women around him die or get hurt." She could feel her frustration growing.

"And I don't want you to be one of them," he said. "Spencer is leaving town. He's spending tonight behind bars. He isn't a threat anymore."

Bridger's logic infuriated her. "Maybe not to me, but what about other women?"

Bridger raked a hand through his hair. "We just keep going around about Spencer.

Did you find proof that he killed any of the women? No. Or proof that he left the other women yellow roses?"

"You can't think it's a coincidence," she snapped.

"I don't know what to think. Frankly I don't want to think about Spencer at all. I want him out of our lives. I want you. I don't want to argue about Spencer. I hate it."

"Then quit defending him!"

"I feel like you put me in this position where I *have* to defend him. Even you admit you have no evidence of any wrongdoing on his part. The police and the sheriff have found nothing. Even if Spencer is leaving you the roses, they don't seem like much of a threat. And now that he's leaving town and right this moment behind bars…"

She shook her head, amazed at how furious she could be with him. He was so damned… fair. But he was wrong. "I don't think we should discuss this anymore tonight."

Bridger relaxed. "Good."

"I have to go."

He groaned. "I wish you'd stay."

She shook her head. "It's best I go." She

turned on her heel and headed down the stairs, through the restaurant and to her car. Her head was spinning. She had needed him to take her side against Spencer. She knew it wasn't fair, but she didn't care.

Worse, she couldn't help thinking about what he'd told her. Her grandmother and the rest of the Whitehorse Sewing Circle had been operating an illegal adoption agency?

It was too bizarre to be believable, and yet she knew Bridger wouldn't have made something like this up. Especially given that apparently the sheriff knew all about it since he was dating Eve.

Laci stopped by the rest home. It was late, but she just needed to see her grandmother. Pearl Cavanaugh's room was dimly lit. Laci stepped in, tiptoeing to the bed. Her grandmother was sleeping peacefully.

Laci bent down to plant a kiss on her cool, dry cheek. As she straightened, she felt tears blur her eyes. If only her grandmother would get better. If only she would be able to talk to Laci again. Laci missed their long talks. If her grandmother really was involved in something before her stroke, Laci knew she would have had her reasons. Laci really needed to hear those reasons.

Once outside again, she climbed in her car and drove the five miles to pull into her lane. The house was dark, the night even blacker. A wind had come up. It whipped the trees around the house and rocked her car as she got out and started toward the porch wishing she'd left a light on.

A coyote howled, making her jump. She glanced toward the Banning ranch. No lights were on. Bridger had told her that Spencer was in jail. She had nothing to worry about.

This time the note was stuck in the door. It dropped to the floor as Laci unlocked the door. Angry, she pushed into the living room, slamming the door behind her as she snapped on a light and ripped open the envelope with *Laci Cherry* printed on the front.

The words written inside shouldn't have shocked her. But they did.

Your mother's body is in the old Cherry house.

Laci dropped the note. It fluttered to the floor to land in a pile of broken glass. She stumbled back in surprise, finally seeing the room in front of her.

It had been ransacked: books thrown to the floor, the couch cushions cut and bleeding stuffing, the lamps upended.

What struck her was that the house hadn't been burglarized—but vandalized instead. This was the work of someone who'd been furious.

She dug her cell phone out of her purse and was making the call to the sheriff when the front door banged open on a gust of wind.

She swung around, dropping the cell phone to snatch up the base of a lamp from an end table where it had been knocked over. She raised it as the door filled with a dark shape. Belatedly she realized that she couldn't have heard anyone drive up over the roar of the wind.

"EASY, IT'S ME," BRIDGER called as Laci started to swing the lamp base, ready to coldcock him.

She dropped the lamp and ran into his arms. He could feel her trembling and near tears as he took in the room beyond her. He knew it wasn't just the ransacked house that had her upset.

After she'd taken off, he'd gone after her, fearing that she might be right about a whole lot of things. It was his fault that he'd let Spencer come between them. His guilt had made him defend Spencer even when he'd had doubts. Worse, he hadn't wanted to believe it. Even about the roses.

But who had done this to her house? Not Spencer—he was in jail. Was it possible he'd done this before Bridger had seen him and called the cops?

Laci pulled back to look up at him, her eyes a liquid blue that threatened to drown him.

"Here, let me do that," he said, taking her cell phone from her. He told the dispatcher what had happened. She patched him through to the sheriff, who told him to sit tight, not touch anything, he was on his way.

Bridger watched Laci kneel down to carefully pick up a note and envelope from the floor.

"The sheriff said not to touch anything," he told her.

"Too late," she said. "This was stuck in the door."

"Let's go wait in my truck." He led her out to his pickup and started the engine to clear the windows.

"This is the third one I've received," she said, handing him the note.

He snapped on the overhead light and read the note twice. "I don't understand."

"Someone has been leaving them for me."

"Why didn't you tell me about this?" he demanded, but her expression made it too clear why. He snapped off the light, pitching them into darkness. The only sound was the engine and the whir of the heater fan. "I'm sorry. I haven't exactly inspired your trust in me, have I?"

The night was mild for November, but only a fool wouldn't know it could snow at any time. This was Montana. Wait ten minutes and the weather would change.

Bridger looked out into the semidarkness. It was too dark to see the outline of the Little Rockies along the horizon. At first he'd missed mountains, but something about the prairie appealed to him. Its terrain appeared flat but was in truth filled with rocky, juniper-thick gullies and ravines. At first it also appeared harsh, barren, but it was neither.

He saw the lights before he heard the wail of the siren. It was going to be a long night—and nothing like he'd planned when he'd asked Laci to dinner.

He drew her to him as they sat on the bench seat of his pickup and waited for the sheriff.

"I need to ask you something," he said as he watched the sheriff's car grow closer. "Did you go through Spencer's house looking for evidence?"

Her eyes widened with surprise. "No. You think *he* did that to my house in retaliation?"

Bridger shrugged. He no longer knew what to think.

"I suppose you know about my parents."

He'd already heard the story and seen the old Cherry house.

"Every kid in town thinks the house is haunted," she said as the wail of the siren grew.

He didn't blame kids for thinking that. The first time he'd seen the house, it had given him an eerie feeling. Finding out that there'd been a murder/suicide in the house had certainly added to that.

"So you don't remember your father's parents?" he asked.

She shook her head. "From what I can gather, we seldom saw them before the… tragedy." She chewed at her lower lip for a moment. "I was too young to remember them. I can't even remember my parents."

"You had your grandparents. I had my adoptive parents," he said. "But it still doesn't keep you from wondering about your real parents, does it?"

"I'm sorry I got so upset earlier," Laci said. "I'll do what I can to help you find your birth mother."

He smiled. "Thanks."

"I know what it's like not knowing your mother. In my case, both of my parents." She sat up straighter as Sheriff Jackson pulled into the yard and cut his lights and engine.

"What is this?" Laci asked as she picked up something from the floorboard.

He looked up to see that she was holding the photo album he'd found in the basement of Doc Holloway's house. He'd tossed it on the seat, but it must have fallen to the floor on the drive out here. Once he'd made up his mind to go after her, he'd been in a hurry, hating the way they'd left things.

Laci snapped on the overhead light and ran her fingers over the cover of the album. He'd pretty much forgotten about finding it, he'd been so busy with the restaurant. And Laci.

She flipped the album open to a page with photographs.

"It's just an old album I—" Her shocked expression stopped him. "You recognize the girls in the photographs?"

Her voice broke as she asked, "Where did you get this?"

"In an old house owned by Dr. Holloway." Was it possible the girls in the photographs were part of the adoption ring, just as he suspected?

He saw that Laci's hands were shaking as she clutched the photo album to her chest, her eyes filling with tears.

"This had to have belonged to my mother. She took the album with her when she left. The photos are of me and my sister Laney."

Chapter Eleven

"Okay, calm down," Sheriff Carter Jackson said as he and Laci and Bridger congregated in his office later that night. "I have forensics coming to go through your house to see what we can find, but I have to tell you, I doubt whoever did that to your house left any fingerprints."

"I'm more concerned about the notes about my mother, especially after discovering this album," Laci said.

Carter nodded. "How can you be so sure it's your mother's, the one she took with her?"

"I remember my grandfather saying it was blue, my mother's favorite color," Laci said. "I'd appreciate it if you wouldn't tell him about it at this point, though. I know how much it's going to upset him."

"I assume for that reason you also haven't mentioned the notes to him?" Carter asked.

She nodded and dropped into a chair across from his desk. "You think they're just a prank, don't you? But what if my mother never left town, just like the note says? What if she's buried in that house?"

"It doesn't explain how her photo album ended up in Dr. Holloway's house either," Bridger pointed out. "Especially given what we know about the doctor's connection to the adoption ring. I told Laci."

Sheriff Jackson didn't look happy to hear that. "Let's not jump to any conclusions."

"Unless Dr. Holloway had something to do with her death," Bridger said.

The sheriff shot Bridger a look. "Let's try to keep to the facts. I'll go out with some men and we'll see what we can find at the house. But let's keep in mind—it's been almost thirty years. If someone around here knew about this, why would they decide to tell you now?"

"I've wondered about that. Maybe the person is dying and has to get this off her conscience," Laci said. "Or maybe she's been gone all these years." She saw the look the sheriff gave her. "It doesn't mean the person doesn't know what she's talking about."

"She?" Carter asked.

"It feels like a woman is writing the notes to me," Laci said and shrugged.

"I did some checking," Carter said. "A friend of your grandmother Cherry's is in the nursing home. The nurses found her in your grandmother Pearl's room."

Laci sat up in alarm. "Is Gramma Pearl all right?"

"She's fine."

"Who is this woman who was a friend of Alma Cherry?"

"Nina Mae Cross."

"Eve Bailey's grandmother?"

Carter nodded. "Nina Mae has Alzheimer's so there's no way she sent you the notes. But there's a chance another woman at the nursing home took it upon herself to do it based on something Nina Mae had been saying."

"And this is the first time you mentioned this to Laci?" Bridger demanded.

Carter sighed. "Given Nina Mae's mental state, there was no reason to suspect that she knows anything about Geneva Cherry's whereabouts. Also, the notes Laci gave me had no fingerprints on them. It is doubtful that an elderly person living at the nursing home would make sure her fingerprints weren't on anything."

"Who was the woman who you think sent the notes?" Bridger asked.

"Bertie Cavanaugh."

"My great-aunt?" Laci said and saw Bridger's surprise.

"I found some stationery in her room that matches that of the notes," Carter said. "But it's a common brand sold at the drugstore in Whitehorse. Meanwhile, we'll search the old Cherry place."

"What are the chances there's something there to find after all these years?" Bridger said. "Laci said kids have played in that old house as far back as she can remember. You would have thought they'd have found anything of interest years ago."

"Unless…" The words caught in Laci's throat. "Unless the body is in the root cellar under the house."

Sheriff Carter shook his head. "Your

grandfather had one of the local masons brick up the entrance years ago."

Rumor was that the root cellar was where her grandfather Cherry had taken his wife and killed her before taking his own life.

"Who does the house belong to?" Bridger asked, frowning.

"It was put up for auction for taxes after the incident," the sheriff said. "There were no offers on it. So I believe it belongs to the county."

"My grandfather had it bricked up after my mother left?" Laci asked, her voice sounding strange to her.

Carter nodded. "We'll reopen it tomorrow. If there is anything down there to find, we'll find it."

"Anyone ever figure out why Cherry did it?" Bridger asked.

"There was no note and no sign of a problem, according to the file I looked up about the deaths," the sheriff said.

Laci rose unsteadily from her chair. "When will you do it?"

"At first light—but I don't want you anywhere near there," Carter said.

She started to argue, but Bridger stepped in. "I'll go," he said more to her than the sheriff. "I'll be there and I'll call you as soon as we know something." He turned to face the sheriff. Laci could see the determined set of his jaw.

Carter looked as if he was going to object but must have seen it would be better than having Laci anywhere nearby. "Okay, Laci. Bridger comes as long as he stays out of the way—and you are nowhere near the place, agreed?"

Laci had no choice but to agree even though she knew she would go crazy until she heard. And she knew that Bridger knew it, as well.

He grabbed her hand and squeezed it as he pulled her to him and gave her a quick kiss, his gaze locking with hers. "Will you be all right alone in my apartment over the restaurant?"

"I'll be fine. Later I'll go down to the restaurant and bake something," she said, holding up the key he'd given her earlier that night.

"Good thinking. Just keep the doors

locked." He turned to the sheriff. "You picked up Spencer this evening for driving under the influence, right?"

Carter nodded.

So Spencer was under lock and key. Now all she had to worry about was what was in the old Cherry house.

The next morning she watched Bridger leave with the sheriff and the deputies in one of the patrol cars, headed for Old Town Whitehorse. It took all her self-control not to follow them, but she knew the sheriff well enough to know he'd meant what he'd said about her staying away.

Carter had allowed Bridger to come along only to keep her away. If she showed up, she was certain the sheriff would send Bridger away, as well.

She was too antsy to stay in the apartment—or even to cook. She decided to go see her grandmother.

AT THE NURSING HOME, her grandmother glanced toward her as she entered. Laci thought Gramma Pearl's eyes brightened, but it could have been just the light.

"Hi, Gramma," she said, taking the chair next to the bed. She was so anxious she feared her grandmother would sense it and it might cause the elderly woman more stress. She shifted her thoughts away from her mother and the old Cherry place and what was going to happen there and thought of Bridger.

Just the thought made her smile. "I think I'm in love." She grinned at her grandmother and thought she saw amusement in Pearl's gaze. "I know—you've heard it all before. Since first grade, huh? But this time, Gramma, I think it's the real thing."

She took her grandmother's hand. "It has me a little worried, though. I wish Laney was here so I'd have someone to talk to about it. Laney's still in Hawaii on her honeymoon."

Laci thought she felt her grandmother squeeze her hand. "Her husband Nick is really wonderful. He's a deputy here in town. They'll be home soon and we'll all be together again."

She just wished they'd be here for Christmas—and the restaurant opening.

"Oh, did I mention…I'm probably going to be working in a restaurant. My catering company didn't exactly take off. I think it was fate, my meeting the owner of a restaurant and a man who loves to cook as much as I do. Bridger Duvall is like no other man I've ever met."

There was no mistaking it: her grandmother's hand tensed. Laci looked into her grandmother's eyes and saw…what? Fear? Panic?

"It's okay, Gramma." Her grandmother's eyes had filled with tears and she seemed to be having trouble breathing.

Laci reached for the nurse's call button, alarmed by her grandmother's reaction.

A nurse came hurrying in. "What happened?"

"I don't know. I was just sitting here talking to her." Laci moved out of the way so the nurse could check her grandmother. "Is she all right?"

"Her pulse is up. She seems upset. Let's let her rest now. Maybe you could come back later."

Laci nodded, backing out of the room.

Her grandmother's eyes followed her, the fear and panic still there.

IT WAS ONE OF THOSE gray days, the clouds low, the light dim like an early dusk.

Bridger stood outside the old, dilapidated Cherry house, huddling against the brisk wind. It was only weeks from Christmas. What snow had fallen in the middle of November had blown into deep drifts that had filled in the barrow pits and piled up like frozen waves beside buildings and fence lines, leaving the rest of the land clear.

One such sculpted drift ran along the lee side of the house and stood a good five feet tall.

He stared out across the wind-scoured land. He'd often wondered what he was doing here. More to the point, why he stayed. As the wind howled along the rotting eave of the house, he thought he knew the answer.

His adoptive mother had sent him here. He'd been lost. Lost and restless. True, he'd felt he didn't know himself and wouldn't until he found out who his birth parents had been.

Whitehorse had just been a stop-gap. He'd never dreamed of staying here when he'd rented the old McAllister place. Now he had a restaurant that would open in a matter of days, even ahead of schedule.

He smiled to himself. He'd never believed in fate. He'd always thought he made his own fate, just as he made his own luck. But if he hadn't come here, he would never have met Laci Cavanaugh.

Behind him, the deputies unloaded the equipment and the cadaver-sniffing dog from the vehicles.

"Just stay out of the way," the sheriff said to him not unkindly.

Bridger nodded and followed the men toward the front steps of the house, standing back as one of the men removed the sheet of plywood covering the door before breaking open the nailed-shut door to shine a light into the darkness inside, then motioning for them to follow.

LACI WAS SHAKEN AS she drove to the restaurant and entered through the back. She couldn't imagine what had upset her grandmother. It wouldn't be like Gramma Pearl to get upset over Laci's change of career plans.

Not after Laci had changed her major at college a half dozen times.

She pulled out a pound of butter and cut it into the mixing bowl. Cookies. She would bake something rich and wonderful for Bridger. She was debating which of her favorite recipes to use when the back door opened and she realized she'd been so upset over her grandmother that she'd failed to lock it.

Spencer Donovan stepped into the kitchen, the door closing behind him. She stared at him in shock.

"I thought you were in jail," she cried, backing toward the knife rack. She grabbed a wide-bladed knife and brandished it front of her. "Stay away from me!"

"Laci, have you gone crazy?" Spencer asked, stopping just inside the kitchen doorway.

"Get out of here or I'm going to call the sheriff."

"The sheriff is down in Old Town and we both know it."

"How did you get out of jail?"

"It pays to have the best lawyer that money can buy," Spencer said, glancing around as if looking for Bridger.

"Bridger will be back any minute," she said.

"No, he won't," Spencer said with a sigh. "He went off with the sheriff down to Old Town." He stepped toward her. "You have everyone suspecting me now. Even Bridger, the one person who was on my side."

"Don't." She held the knife in front of her. "Don't come any closer."

He stopped and shook his head as if confused. "Why don't you listen to what I'm telling you? I didn't hurt them. I loved them. It wasn't me. If this doesn't stop…" His look appeared filled with worry. "It's not safe."

She stared at him, fear making her heart thunder in her chest. The knife in her hand began to shake as a tremor moved through her. Spencer was sick, just as she'd suspected. Why else would he hurt the women he'd supposedly loved? She gripped the knife tighter and stepped toward him. "Get out."

His gaze focused on the knife blade. He took a step back. "I never wanted anyone to get hurt. You have to believe me. I'm leaving town. I just wanted to see you and warn you to stop talking to people about me. If you don't, you're going to end up like the others." He mumbled the last words as he backed toward the door.

She waited until she heard the back door close before she rushed to lock it, shaking from her encounter and more convinced than ever that Spencer Donovan was a dangerous man.

THE POSTER ON THE front door warned trespassers would be prosecuted. Bridger followed the others through the open door into the house.

The smell as he stepped inside wasn't just that of a closed-up house, that old, musty, vacant odor. This scent was one of decay.

Bridger glanced over at the sheriff and saw his face was tightened with dread.

There were piles of old clothes and broken pieces of furniture. The woodstove looked as if it had been used in the last thirty years, which meant a vagrant could have been staying here at one time. Or local kids had been using the place as a hideout.

"Watch for rattlesnakes," Carter said as they moved across once-sealed hardwood floors that were now grayed and buckled with age and water and ruin.

The smell of the house was bad enough. And while he wasn't afraid of rattlesnakes, Bridger also didn't much like surprising one, either.

His biggest fear was that they would find Laci's mother's body in this horrible old house. If a place could harbor evil, it was these four walls.

He didn't need anyone to tell him that something horrible had happened here. He could feel it. Just as he could imagine old man Cherry taking his wife down to the root cellar. She had to have known what he'd planned to do.

It didn't help either that Bridger had never liked small, dark places. His aversion stemmed from being accidentally locked in a trunk while playing with some neighbor kids when he was five.

They searched the upper floors of the house first, then one of the deputies opened the basement door. A wave of stale, freezing, putrid air wafted up. Bridger saw the deputy look to the sheriff.

"I'll go first," Sheriff Jackson said, and the rest of them followed him down the creaking wooden stairs, flashlights bobbing into the dark hole of the floorless basement and root cellar.

Bridger was only thankful that Laci would never have to come down here.

The basement was full of junk. He thought he heard something slither away into a dark corner. Mice?

To one side of the basement was an opening that he assumed had once led to the infamous root cellar. The opening had been bricked in.

"Let's open it up," the sheriff said, and two of the deputies removed sledgehammers from their gear and went to work.

The sound of steel against stone echoed like gunshots through the cold, still basement.

Bridger stood back, praying they wouldn't

find anything but fearing they would. No one knew why the Cherrys had died down here. Not even the closest neighbors could know what went on behind closed doors.

Marriages were never as they appeared from the outside. He thought of his own parents. He'd never heard them raise their voices in anger toward each other. Their love for each other gave him strength but also set the bar so high he'd feared he would never have that kind of relationship. Until Laci.

Except he wasn't his father's son. He'd always feared he would never measure up to his father. He didn't have his adoptive mother's forgiving heart or his adoptive father's calm, cool disposition. And for a very good reason, as it turned out.

The pounding stopped. The bricks lay in rubble beneath a huge dark hole large enough to climb through.

Carter handed him a flashlight and ordered one of the men to remain there. The other deputies picked up shovels and stepped through the hole after the sheriff. Bridger followed the cadaver dog.

The first thing that hit him was the smell

of something dead. He'd grown up on a ranch, and it was a smell he knew only too well.

He took shallow breaths as he moved along the wooden shelves filled with dozens of dusty quart jars, the contents murky and indiscernible. Bridger swore under his breath. What a horrible place to die.

Ahead, the sheriff and two deputies had stopped at a spot where the dirt floor rose in a hump like that of a grave. The dog was already there, leaving little doubt as to what they would find.

A deputy turned up a spade full of dirt. Bridger heard the shovel strike something on the second attempt and watched with dread as the blade turned up the first bone.

Chapter Twelve

"The remains are that of a male, late twenties or early thirties, and they definitely haven't been there thirty years," Carter said when Laci arrived at the sheriff's office. "It's not your mother."

Laci dropped into a chair and closed her eyes, fighting tears. "Then why would someone send me those stupid notes?"

The sheriff shook his head. "I can only assume the person knew about the bones and thought they were your mother's. We found another entrance to the basement from the outside that has been used since the root cellar was bricked up."

"That would explain the lights people have said they've seen inside the house," Laci said.

Carter nodded. "Clearly there's been someone using the old house. From some of the paraphernalia we found, it appears to be drug users."

"If the bones aren't my mother's, then whose are they?" she asked, drawn back to what had been found in the old Cherry house.

"I'll know more after I get the results from the crime lab," Carter said. "I'm checking missing-persons reports now. The coroner says the remains have been in the root cellar for under ten years."

"What can we do if Spencer hasn't left town?" Bridger asked. "I don't want him threatening Laci again."

"Unfortunately, the way this works is unless he breaks the law, there isn't much we can do," Carter said. "Laci can get a restraining order against him—"

"A piece of paper isn't going to keep Spencer away from her," Bridger snapped.

The sheriff nodded. "If he contacts you again, Laci, I'll have him picked up. But you've seen how long I was able to hold him the last time. Unless he commits a crime…"

"What about the photo album Bridger found in Dr. Holloway's house?" she asked, thinking of her mother.

"We checked the house, Laci, but it's been thirty years. Any evidence that might have been there is long gone. We didn't find anything. I'm sorry."

"Why would the album be there?" She knew what she wanted him to tell her. She needed a good explanation for her mother leaving the album in an old house in Whitehorse—an explanation other than her mother leaving it behind because she never left town alive.

He shook his head. "Your guess is as good as mine, I'm afraid. I really think you should talk to your grandfather about it. There might be some simple explanation."

She got to her feet and Bridger followed suit. She wished she could go back to believing her mother was alive and living somewhere far from here.

"Well, thank you for letting me know about the bones you found." She wished she knew what to feel.

Bridger put his arm around her as they

left. "I'm not letting you out of my sight until Spencer is gone for good," he said once they were outside.

She rested her cheek against her chest. "Sounds good to me."

BRIDGER AND LACI spent the next few weeks getting the restaurant ready for its grand opening.

Bridger was relieved that there had been no sign of Spencer. At Laci's insistence, the sheriff was doing more digging into Spencer's past, talking to Patty Waring and others. Laci's biggest fear was that Spencer would trap another woman in his deadly snare.

Bridger convinced himself that Spencer would lay low for a while. He would know that he was being investigated even further. That alone worried Bridger, though. He'd seen how upset Spencer had been when he knew that Laci thought he was a killer. Why else had he stopped by yet another time to warn her off?

But the fear that the investigation would make Spencer return to Whitehorse waned as the days passed. Bridger was starting to believe they would never see Spencer again.

As the grand opening night of the restaurant drew near, the town of Whitehorse took on the look of the coming Christmas holiday. Bright colored lights adorned the town square, shops sported dancing Santas and snowmen and Christmas music played on the town's only radio station from morning until night.

Bridger found himself getting into the holiday spirit. He'd anguished over finding the perfect gift for Laci for weeks now. At his insistence, she'd moved into the apartment over the restaurant with him. That way she was always close by—usually right there in the large restaurant kitchen with him as they planned every detail for opening night.

Her grandfather Titus hadn't taken the news well—even after Laci had explained about Spencer. But Titus has been cordial enough since then, and Bridger had begun to think everything might work out yet.

Spencer was gone if not forgotten. Bridger's dream of a restaurant was about to come true. And then there was Laci…. He smiled to himself at the thought of her.

They spent much of their time either cooking or upstairs in his bed, making love. Their lovemaking went beyond touch, beyond desire, beyond pleasure. They came together as if it had been destined long before they were born.

It seemed too good to be true.

He feared that someone would come along and take it away from him. Spencer Donovan, perhaps.

Just as his mother had taken away his idyllic memories of childhood when she'd told him he'd been lied to about who he was.

"You look worried."

He glanced up to see Laci standing across the kitchen, studying him.

"Is it about opening night?" she asked.

"No, it's nothing," he assured her as he stepped to her, taking her in his arms. "It's nothing, really."

LACI KNEW HE HAD TO BE nervous. All this work and finally here it was—opening night.

She wouldn't have given anything for the time they'd spent together getting the restaurant ready. The days had flown by as if in a dream. And now, finally, it was opening night. She was determined that nothing would spoil this for Bridger.

Laci had been baking cookies for several days now and freezing them for the holidays. She would miss her sister and Maddie. Christmas wouldn't be the same. But she would be spending the holidays with Bridger and she was crazy about him. So it would all be fine.

She realized as she leaned into Bridger that she hadn't thought of Spencer in a long time. She felt a stab of guilt. That also meant she hadn't thought about Alyson. She knew she'd done everything she could. Not that it had helped.

"Don't worry," she told Bridger. "Tonight will be a night you'll never forget."

He chuckled. "Let's hope that's because it's a success and not a disaster."

"Oh, don't be silly. With my desserts, how can it miss?" she joked.

He drew back to look at her. "I know I should wait until Christmas…"

She felt her heart kick up a beat.

"…but I have a little something for you."

He reached into his pocket and pulled out a small red envelope.

Her fingers trembled as she took it.

"This is just the first part of your Christmas present."

She smiled uneasily as she ripped open the envelope and took out the single sheet of folded red paper. A check fluttered to the floor, dropping like her heart. "My paycheck?" She'd thought they were in this together. Now she realized he saw her as just an employee. And a lover.

"Read the note," he said as if sensing her disappointment.

She read the note. Twice. "You want me to be your partner in the restaurant?" Her voice broke.

"I do. The check is for all your work. I know you have your heart set on your own catering business, but I hope you'll take my offer."

She didn't know what to say. Or to feel. "I need to think this over." She couldn't help her surprise. Or her disappointment. What had she expected? A proposal of a different kind? It was way too soon. He was offering her half of his restaurant, Northern Lights.

But as the rest of the staff came in to get ready for the opening, she knew what she really wanted Bridger to offer her was his heart.

Sheriff Carter Jackson got the call at home as he was getting ready to go pick up Eve for the grand opening of her brother's restaurant.

"Sheriff? It's Deputy Ryan. We just found Glen Whitaker."

Something in his deputy's voice warned Carter that the news wasn't good.

"It appears he was bludgeoned to death with a shovel," the deputy said, taking Carter by surprise. He'd expected a car accident. Or a heart attack. Anything but murder. And as the days had passed, he'd started thinking maybe Glen had just up and left town.

Carter swore under his breath. "Where?"

"Found him and his vehicle out behind a barn at the McAllister place. I'd say, from the looks of him, he's been here for a while. Also, we found his camera. It was stuffed into some hay bales behind the barn for some reason."

"Don't let anyone touch the camera. I'll

call the coroner and meet you out there." Carter hung up, still shocked, and called Eve to tell her he was going to be more than late. And he'd been so looking forward to tonight. In fact, he'd planned to pop the question after dinner.

"It's fine," she said when he reached her. "McKenna is home. She'd love to go with me. Meet us there if you can."

As Carter drove toward Old Town White-horse, he wondered what Glen had been doing at the old McAllister place. And where had Bridger Duvall been at the time? For weeks Bridger had been living in the apartment over the restaurant with Laci Cavanaugh. And the hidden camera? None of it made any sense. But then, murder was often senseless.

He told himself that no way did Bridger have anything to do with this. Unfortunately, Glen had been killed on property being rented by Bridger. Still, why would Bridger want to kill Glen? Why would anyone want to kill Glen, for that matter?

Carter just hoped that Eve's brother had an airtight alibi.

LACI PEEKED THROUGH the swinging doors to see Bridger shaking hands with the patrons. She glowed with pride. Bridger had done it. Northern Lights was a huge success.

Bridger spotted her almost as if he'd sensed her there, almost as if he'd missed her. He smiled, a smile that was so brilliant it was blinding, and motioned for her to join him.

She nodded but didn't move as other departing guests called him over so they could congratulate him. Dinner had been over for some time, but many of the locals had hung around even after the help had cleared the dishes and cleaned the kitchen and left.

Laci loved seeing the way the town was supporting the restaurant and Bridger. She felt as if she would bust with happiness, and the thought came pouring out of her as if from some deep well of emotion inside her.

She loved him.

She *loved* Bridger Duvall.

Not like the other times she'd been in love. This time was different.

The realization should have panicked her.

Would have panicked her if she'd had more than an instant to think it.

An arm circled her waist, drawing her back from the door at the same instant a cloth was clamped over her mouth.

She drew a breath to scream but only managed to draw in the sickening smell of the chemical on the cloth.

The room began to swim. She tried to fight off her attacker, but it was useless. As she was being pulled toward the back door, she blindly grabbed at the counter for something to use as a weapon to defend herself.

She knocked over the pitcher of sweetened cream, felt the stickiness, and then her fingers were in one of the leftover tortes. She'd know that texture anywhere. Just as she knew who her attacker had to be. She frantically tried to write the first letter of his name in the surface of the torte as she was dragged backward.

She felt her body go limp from whatever drug she'd been given. The last she remembered was the dark alley and the slamming of a car door.

LIGHTS GLOWED BEHIND the old barn on the McAllister place as Sheriff Carter Jackson pulled up.

He'd seen a lot of crime scenes, but this one struck him as more than a little unusual given that the killer had simply dropped the murder weapon beside the body.

"Wrap that shovel carefully," Carter ordered. "I want to check it right away for fingerprints." He glanced at the barn wall and Glen Whitaker's vehicle. There were footprints in the soft dirt—Glen's boots and a smaller shoe. The killer's? If so, the killer had very small feet—small enough to be a woman's.

Carter noted the uneven ground between the vehicle and the barn. On closer inspection he saw where someone had laid a hand on the outside of the car for balance. "Get the prints off here, as well. I'll take them in myself." He turned to see his deputy waiting with a small camera bag. "Let's see those photographs."

Carter took the digital camera back to his patrol car and turned it on. Instantly he saw that the camera was indeed Glen Whitaker's.

There were numerous shots of Alice Miller's ninetieth birthday party and shots of Alyson Banning Donovan's funeral.

He flipped through them quickly, anxious to see the last photographs that Glen had taken, hoping there would be a clue as to who killed him. Like the camera, Glen's vehicle had been hidden behind the barn. Also, given where Glen's body had been found, it followed to reason Glen himself had been hiding back there. But why?

Carter was disappointed when he reached the end of the photographs. There was nothing before the funeral. He swore and went back through the photographs, stopping on an image of a woman in the background at the funeral.

There were several more photographs of the woman. Glen had zoomed in on her, snapping a shot as the woman made what appeared to be a hurried getaway. Why was that?

Carter had never seen the woman before. So what was Glen's interest in her?

The last shot at the funeral was of

Spencer. He seemed to be going after the mystery woman.

A deputy tapped on the window. "I have those prints ready for you to take."

Carter raced back to town with the prints and the photographs. While he ran the prints, he called Mark Sanders and asked him to stop by.

"I've never seen the woman before," Sanders said. "I have no idea why Glen would have taken shots of her."

"She and Spencer Donovan were the last people photographed before Glen Whitaker was murdered," he told the newspaperman.

BRIDGER GLANCED BACK toward the kitchen, disappointed Laci hadn't joined him. Darn the woman. It was just like her to think it would steal his thunder.

The night had been an unmitigated success. He couldn't believe it. He felt as if he were floating on air. His own restaurant.

But tonight would have meant nothing without Laci. And now that it was almost over, all he wanted to do was share the rest of the night with her.

Earlier, he'd seen the expression on her face when he'd offered her the partnership in Northern Lights. He'd thought she would be pleased. But she'd seemed disappointed. He hoped he could explain later, explain what he was really offering her.

Most of the guests were leaving. He said his goodbyes.

As he pushed open the doors to the kitchen, he was shocked and disappointed to see that the room was empty. No Laci.

The back door was partially ajar. He went to it and looked out. The alley was also empty. Upstairs, he called for her, but she wasn't anywhere around.

Back in the kitchen, he started to worry. She'd left without saying goodbye? She must have been more hurt than he'd thought. Sometimes he was such a fool.

He turned and glanced back at the kitchen. One of her chocolate tortes was sitting on the edge of the counter. Something looked odd about it.

He stepped to the torte and let out a curse when he saw that someone had ruined the smooth surface.

Who would do such a thing? Laci? Had she left mad?

But as he stared down at the torte he saw that the marred surface was in the shape of a letter. An *S*.

His heart began to pound harder as he looked around and noticed that Laci had left her purse and her car keys in the cupboard where she'd put them earlier in case she had to run out and get any last-minute items.

She couldn't have left without them. Then where was she?

As he started to step toward the back door again, the sole of his shoe stuck to the floor. Something sticky had been spilled there.

He reached down and felt the white, sticky substance, then stood and checked the counter. There'd been some clotted cream in a container next to the last torte when he'd gone out to bid the guests a good-night.

The container was empty, the cream drying on one side where it had been spilled.

That's when he noticed that the cupboard by the back door was ajar. He stepped to it, fear rising in his chest as he pulled open the door. At first nothing looked out of place.

Then he saw that the box of matches he kept next to the emergency candles was gone.

What the hell had happened back here after he'd left?

He looked back toward the spilled cream and saw the marks where something had been dragged across the cream-sticky floor.

The sight set his heart racing.

The drag marks led out the back door and into the dark alley.

Bridger was reaching for his cell phone to call the sheriff when he looked up and saw a figure silhouetted in the kitchen doorway. *"Spencer?"*

Chapter Thirteen

"Where's Laci?" Bridger demanded, snapping shut the phone to launch himself at Spencer. He grabbed him by the collar, driving him back into the wall. "Where the hell is she? If anything has happened to her—"

"I swear to you I haven't done anything to her," Spencer cried, his eyes wide, terrified. "You have to believe me."

"I'm through believing you. I should have listened to Laci. She tried to warn me. She told me about the damned roses you were leaving her." He tightened his grip on Spencer, seeing the fear in his eyes, a fear much deeper than what Bridger might do to him.

Bridger stepped back and looked at him,

seeing how disheveled he was, how unnerved. "What the hell is going on?"

"I warned Laci," Spencer cried, his voice breaking. "I told her to quit snooping around in my past. I knew this was going to happen. That's why I came back."

Bridger stared at Spencer, his heart thundering in his chest, his blood roaring in his ears. "What are you talking about?"

"She's not dead."

The words rocked Bridger back on his heels. "She better not be dead."

"Not Laci. Emma."

"Emma?" Spencer was talking nonsense. Was he drunk again? "Emma Shane?"

"She's not dead," Spencer repeated.

"That's crazy. We saw her in the house right before it blew up."

Spencer was shaking his head, his face still chalky, beads of sweat breaking out on his forehead. "I'm telling you, she didn't die in the fire. I've *seen* her. I couldn't tell anyone because I knew they'd think I was crazy, but I saw her at the reception."

Bridger stared at him openmouthed. "Your *wedding* reception?"

"That had to be the look Laci said she saw. I just glanced up and there Emma was. But then I blinked and she wasn't there and I thought I just imagined her." Spencer put his face in his hands for a moment before looking up at Bridger again. "It wasn't the first time. I've seen her before. I thought it was just the nightmares. You remember the horrible nightmares I had after...." He rushed on, the words tumbling out. "She looks different. Her hair is long and some-times it's dark brown and other times it's blond or red or—"

"You've lost your mind," Bridger said, grabbing him again. Spencer was crazy. It was the only explanation. "You're the one who took Laci. She left an *S* in the top of the torte as you were dragging her out. Now what the hell did you do with her?"

"It wasn't me," he managed to rasp. "I swear to you. It was Emma." His eyes locked with Bridger's. "She drowned Alyson and killed the others. I know that now. When Laci told me about the yellow roses…" He broke down.

Bridger let go of him, remembering what

Laci had told him about the other women in Spencer's life. Spencer was much sicker than Bridger could have imagined. "You need help."

"See?" Spencer said, his voice breaking. "This is why I didn't tell anyone about her." His face crumbled. "Don't you see, if she's been leaving Laci yellow roses, then Laci is next."

Bridger's blood ran cold. "What do you mean *next?*"

"Emma's going to kill her—just like the others."

LACI WOKE, HEAD ACHING, sick to her stomach. The car rocked on what felt like a gravel road. She tried to sit up and felt her head swoon.

Where was she? She couldn't remember anything.

Her eyes blinked open, then closed, her lids too heavy to keep open. She tried again and saw that she was in the backseat of a car that was speeding along a gravel road. Her hands and feet were bound with duct tape, and there was a French Canadian station on the radio.

She felt groggy as she pushed herself up until she could see that she was in a large SUV. A woman with long, dark hair was driving. Past her was nothing but darkness, the SUV's headlights cutting a golden swath into it.

"Oh, dear," said the driver, glancing in the rearview mirror. "She's awake."

Before Laci could react, the woman swiveled in the driver's seat and jabbed a syringe into her arm.

"You really need your rest, dear," Laci heard the woman say as the car swerved and Laci tumbled to the floorboard behind the front seats.

In an instant she felt the drug coursing through her veins. The rear of the car blurred. She struggled to get up, but she no longer had control of her limbs. Her body seemed to liquify. She fought to try to keep her eyes open, but it was a losing battle—one she lost quickly.

BRIDGER TRIED NOT TO panic. Laci couldn't have been gone long. If Spencer had taken her, then he couldn't have taken her far. And

Bridger had to believe that was the case given that Emma Shane was dead—and Laci had left an *S* shape in the top of the torte as she was being dragged out of the kitchen.

"Where is your car?" Bridger demanded as he opened the safe he kept under the kitchen counter and took out the .357 Magnum along with a box of cartridges.

"Out front, but Laci isn't—" Spencer looked from the gun to Bridger, then lurched into the bathroom. Bridger heard him retching, then keening like a wounded animal. Bridger waited, then opened the door and dragged Spencer out, wondering what had happened to that older boy who, in an act of heroism, had saved Bridger's life that day in the creek.

"Come on, we're going to find her. You're going to take me to her."

"If you want to find Laci, if you want to save her, you have to believe me. Emma has her." He looked as if he might break down again. "I don't know what she plans to do with her. I swear."

Spencer looked terrified and confused. Dead or alive, Emma Shane had been haunting him for years. Bridger thought of the bad luck Spencer had experienced with women over the years. As Laci had said, no one had that much bad luck. Crazy or not, Spencer was Bridger's only hope of finding Laci and saving her. If it wasn't too late.

"Emma can't be caught. Or stopped," Spencer said in a small voice.

"Like hell," Bridger snapped. "Because you're going to help me find her." But even as he said it, he thought of the big open country of this part of Montana. Laci could be anywhere. Was he really starting to believe that Spencer might be telling the truth?

Bridger reached for Spencer, afraid of what he might do to him but stopped as he caught sight of the cupboard that he'd found open earlier. The only thing missing, he remembered, was a large box of matches.

His heart leaped to his throat. "Fire. Oh, God. I think I know where Laci is," he said as he grabbed hold of Spencer and shoved him toward the door.

THE COMPUTER SCREEN on Sheriff Carter Jackson's desk flashed. He stared at what came up, blinking in disbelief, then shock. The prints matched. He had his killer.

But this couldn't be right. According to the fingerprint analysis, the print taken from the side of Glen Whitaker's vehicle belonged to a woman who'd been dead for twenty years.

Maybe even stranger, the name sounded familiar.

Emma Shane.

It came to him in a rush. Emma Shane, the woman who'd killed herself and her family after Spencer Donovan had broken up with her in high school.

Emma Shane was *alive?*

He sat for a moment, trying to understand what this meant. Emma Shane must have seen Glen Whitaker taking her photograph at the cemetery and followed him out to the old McAllister place. Who knew what Glen might have been doing out there.

So she kills him—but doesn't find the camera with the photographs.

But what was she doing in Old Town Whitehorse to start with? Spencer. Spencer had gone after the woman in the photograph Glen had taken. Spencer knew she was alive.

Carter leaned back in his chair, trying to make sense of this. If Emma Shane was alive and she'd killed Glen to keep her secret—

Laci. Laci had been doing her own investigating. Who knew what she might have turned up by now? Was it possible she'd found out that Emma Shane was alive and doing…what?

Carter sucked in a breath as an answer came to him.

Killing people.

He grabbed his hat and keys and drove over to Duvall's restaurant, only to find the place empty. Laci's car was there, but no sign of Duvall's pickup—or Duvall.

What worried him was that the restaurant door was unlocked, the lights still on. It looked as if they'd left in a hurry.

As Carter was leaving, he noticed that something sticky had been spilled on the kitchen floor.

His concern increased measurably. Getting on his radio in his patrol car, he put out a call to all law enforcement to pull Duvall over if sighted. Also Laci Cavanaugh.

280 The Mystery Man of Whitehorse

The radio squawked the moment he put it down.

"It's Bridger Duvall."

"Patch him through," the sheriff said, already fearing what he was going to hear.

"Laci's missing. I have Spencer and we're headed for Old Town. He swears he had nothing to do with this—"

"Bridger, we found Glen Whitaker murdered behind the barn on the old McAllister place. It looks as if Emma Shane killed him."

Bridger swore. "I'm on my way to Laci's house. I have a bad feeling—"

"I'm right behind you," the sheriff said as he turned on his siren and sped toward Old Town Whitehorse.

BRIDGER DROVE TOO fast, his mind racing, his heart lodged in his throat. He tried not to think about how much of a head start Emma had on them. Or that he might be wrong about where Laci had been taken. That Emma had another plan for Laci, something even more diabolical.

Spencer sat in the passenger seat of his

pickup looking shell-shocked. He hadn't said a word since Bridger had told him what the sheriff had said.

Emma Shane was alive.

Outside the pickup, the night blew past. The road south ran through open country, the sky as starless as the land was treeless.

As he came over a hill, his headlights caught on the old Whitehorse city-limits sign. It was so weathered and worn he could barely make out the lettering. The sign listed to the right, its base surrounded by tumble-weeds.

Bridger blew through Old Town, taking the curve by the old Cherry house hard. Just a little farther. He raced toward the dark horizon and Laci's house just over the next few hills, praying he wouldn't be too late.

As he came over the last rise, he stared in the direction of Laci's house, holding his breath. No orange glow. No flames shooting upward in the sky. He felt weak with relief.

He remembered the day he'd followed the smell of the smoke to Emma's house. He'd been several blocks away when he'd heard the crackle of the flames devouring the dry wooden structure. He'd never forgotten that sound mingled with the shriek of sirens and, closer, the cries of neighbors.

Spencer said he'd seen Emma standing at a second-floor window, backlit by flames, when the propane tank next door had exploded and the house had disintegrated before their eyes.

"How is it possible Emma is alive?" Spencer said next to him.

Bridger glanced over at him, seeing the terror in his eyes. For twenty years Spencer had lived with Emma's ghost. He must have thought himself insane. Even now he didn't want to believe she was alive. Neither did Bridger, because he was certain she had Laci.

Bridger turned down the road to Laci's house, careening into the yard and jumping out of the pickup.

He ran up the steps of the porch, realizing that there was no car in the yard. No one was here. Behind him, he heard Spencer get out of the pickup.

There was a small light burning at the back of the house. As he ran into the living room, he noticed that nothing seemed out of place—not like the time he'd found Laci here and the place ransacked.

In fact, the house looked so normal his heart sank. He *had* guessed wrong about where Laci had been taken. It didn't appear that a criminally insane woman had kidnapped her and brought her here.

But as he raced into the kitchen, he caught the glint of chrome through the back window. There was a car parked out behind the house.

He turned and ran for the stairs, remembering what Spencer had said about seeing Emma standing in the upstairs window of her house just before the explosion.

He hadn't gone far up the stairs when he smelled the nostril-burning reek of gasoline and heard a sickening thud overhead.

LACI'S EYES FLUTTERED as she hit the floor and came to. She looked up, trying to focus not only her eyes but also her brain.

Where was she? Her bedroom? That made no sense. How had she gotten here? She couldn't remember anything but feeling sick.

Her eyes focused on a point over her. A woman's face came into view. The woman looked vaguely familiar.

But what was the woman doing here? And what was that smell? Laci wrinkled her nose and tried to sit up. The woman had a smile on her face, but something definitely wasn't right.

Laci couldn't remember anything for a moment except getting ready for opening night at the restaurant. But now she was home, in her bedroom?

Suddenly a chunk of memory dropped into place. Spencer! He'd grabbed her from behind at the restaurant and dragged her out.

"Where is he?" Laci asked, her voice scratchy. What had he covered her mouth with? Something that had left her tongue cottony. Her arm was sore. She had a vague memory of someone giving her a shot, but it was all jumbled in her aching head. "Where is Spencer?"

"Don't worry about Spencer," she said. "You don't have to concern yourself with him anymore."

Was it possible this woman had saved her?

It's the only thing that made sense. "Have we met before?"

"We've seen each other around. We spoke at the wedding."

The brunette who'd been standing by the back door of the community center as Laci had run out. She remembered her now.

"How did I get here?" Laci asked, feeling as if her head was full of cobwebs. She remembered being grabbed at the restaurant, but everything else was a jumble.

"You don't remember the drive out?"

Laci shook her head and stopped at once, feeling nauseous.

"I brought you up here." The woman was looking at her strangely, studying her appraisingly. "I had to take care of you."

"After Spencer kidnapped me at the restaurant."

The woman smiled. "Yes, Spencer. It's a good thing I've been watching out for you."

A ripple of worry washed over Laci. "You've been watching me?" She remembered feeling as if she was being watched down in Roundup, but that couldn't be what the woman was talking about.

She reached up to rub her hand over her face and saw her wrists were chafed from being taped together. She frowned, trying to remember Spencer doing that.

"I always watch out for the women Spencer gets involved with," the woman said, making Laci look up in surprise.

"I'm not involved with Spencer," Laci said with a frown.

"Aren't you? Has a day gone by that you haven't thought about him? That you haven't tried to find out things about him?" The woman's voice became strident. "That you haven't kept digging and digging, even when he'd left town?"

Her chest constricted. "How do you know Spencer?"

"Spencer and I go way back." The brunette smiled as she picked up a red can from the floor that Laci hadn't noticed before. Laci caught the strong odor of gasoline. "I'm the woman he killed twenty years ago."

Laci stared at the woman, comprehension coming slowly.

"That's right," the woman said with a laugh as she read Laci's expression. "I'm

Emma Shane." With that, she poured the contents of the can onto Laci.

Laci let out a shriek as the cold, foul-smelling fuel soaked her to the skin. She tried to get away but couldn't, her muscles refusing to work.

"Why are you doing this?" Laci cried as the gas fumes burned her eyes.

"Making sure Spencer suffers as much as I have," the woman said, putting down the fuel can and pulling a large box of wooden matches from her jacket pocket. She cocked her heard as she heard what Laci did. Footfalls on the stairs.

"Help!" Laci called. "Help!"

The woman smiled as she took out a cigarette and struck a match, the flame glowing brightly.

BRIDGER RACED UP THE stairs, the .357 Magnum clutched in his hand, the stench of gasoline growing stronger and stronger.

He was almost to the top when he heard Laci call for help.

"We're up here. In Laci's room," a female voice said. "You're just in time."

Behind him, Bridger heard Spencer coming up the stairs.

At the end of the hallway, Bridger aimed the weapon into the room as he came around the open doorway.

He froze at the sight of Laci huddled on the floor, soaking wet, the room reeking of gasoline and a woman with long, dark hair standing over her, holding a lit match to the end of her cigarette.

He took in the scene, his heart in his throat.

Emma Shane. He could see that she'd had reconstructive surgery. But the eyes were the same, and enough of her facial features were intact that there was no doubt who he was looking at.

"Hello, Bridger," she said, smiling as she blew out the match and took a puff on her cigarette, sounding as if they were meeting over cocktails at a party. "It's been a long time."

Not nearly long enough, he thought.

He shifted his gaze to Laci, wanting desperately to tell her not to worry, everything was going to be all right.

But he knew better. All Emma had to do

was drop that cigarette and this room would explode, going up in a flash of flames. Bridger knew he would never be able to get to Laci in time.

He looked into her wide blue eyes. "It's okay, Laci."

Her gaze said she knew better, but she wasn't going to argue the point. He saw her try to move her limbs and wondered what Emma had done to her.

"Emma."

Bridger turned at the sound of Spencer's voice next to him.

Spencer stepped past him and into the room. Bridger reached for him but couldn't stop him.

Emma's smile slipped at the sight of Spencer. "Don't come any closer," she said, holding the cigarette over Laci. "You wouldn't want another woman to suffer because of you, now would you, Spencer?"

Spencer stopped and Bridger stepped up beside him, afraid of what Spencer might do. He wasn't himself. But then, Bridger suspected he hadn't been for some time.

"What's going on, Emma?" Bridger tried to keep the panic out of his voice.

"It has to end here tonight," she said, sounding tired. "I can't do this anymore."

"Don't do it now," Bridger said. "Spencer isn't worth it."

Emma smiled ruefully. "So you finally figured that out. All these years he let you think he jumped into that creek to save you. But I saw the whole thing. Spencer fell in. He didn't mean to save you. He was only trying to save himself."

Bridger glanced over at Spencer. He looked like a sleepwalker, dazed, disconnected.

"Did he tell you that I was pregnant?" Emma asked. "That was why Spencer broke up with me. My father would have killed me if he'd found out, not to mention the disgrace in a small town like Roundup. Spencer used me, then discarded me. He ruined my life— and I've spent the last twenty years ruining his."

LACI SHIFTED ON THE floor. She could feel her limbs again but feared her muscles would fail her if she tried anything. But she couldn't just sit here.

She could hear the desperation and desolation in Emma Shane's voice. This was where it would end—and end badly. She tried to move her body a little more, working not to draw attention to the movement. Emma was focused on Spencer and Bridger, but as the cigarette burned down, Laci knew time was also running out.

And if Bridger tried to get to her before Emma dropped the cigarette, he would be caught in the flames, as well.

"You should leave," Laci said from the floor. "Both of you just get out of here."

"No," Emma snapped. "They have to stay. I want them to see this. I planned this ending. That's why I took the matches and left the cupboard open. If you hadn't figured out where I'd taken Laci, I would have called to tell you. I want Spencer to suffer the way he made me suffer."

Spencer looked as if he was suffering. "You killed them."

Emma laughed. "Did you think you just had bad luck when it came to women? You always were a fool."

The words fell over Laci. Even with her

mind still foggy, she understood. Emma had killed the women in Spencer's life. Emma had killed Alyson.

She felt a bolt of adrenaline shoot through her. She pressed her palms to the floor as she slipped her feet back. Her legs felt too weak, but in her fury she forced her feet under her. Emma must have heard her as Laci shoved herself to her feet. She slammed into Emma, driving her forward toward Spencer and Bridger.

Spencer seemed to come out of his trance as Laci suddenly shot to her feet. He lunged for the gun in Bridger's hand. A shot boomed as Bridger shoved him aside and grabbed for Emma and the glowing cigarette.

It all happened in an instant. Bridger grabbed Emma's hand holding the cigarette and twisted cruelly. Emma screamed in pain as he ripped it from her fingers and shoved her aside to reach for Laci.

Everything seemed to stop as Bridger dragged Laci out, extinguishing the cigarette before wrapping her shivering body in his arms.

As he glanced back into the room, he saw Emma's face, the smile on her lips, as she struck a match. Spencer charged the woman in a rage. Just as he reached her, Emma dropped the lit match. It hit the floor just as Spencer barreled into her, driving her back into the gas-soaked corner of the room.

Emma's smile broadened as she wrapped her arms around Spencer, taking him down with her as the room exploded into a blaze of fire.

Bridger swept Laci, still soaked in gas, down the stairs and out into the cold December night. Behind them, the whole house went up, lighting the night as sirens wailed in the distance.

LACI STOOD UNDER THE hot spray of the shower. Bridger had stripped off her gas-soaked clothing and his own and climbed into the shower with her, holding her trembling body.

She thought she would never be warm again. The last thing she remembered before the ride into Whitehorse to his apartment over the restaurant was looking back to see the house in flames. She'd closed her eyes at the thought of Emma and Spencer in there, their arms wrapped around each other like lovers as flames devoured them.

"I'm so sorry," Bridger whispered as he gently soaped the gas from her skin. "If I'd just listened to you…"

She touched a finger to his lips and shook her head. "I was wrong about Spencer."

"We were both wrong about Spencer." She heard the bitterness in his voice, the pain. "He knew about Emma, but in his fear and his guilt he did nothing."

"Did he know? Or was he like the rest of us, hoping that he was wrong, hoping he could find happiness?" She shook her head. "We're all weak. We're all afraid."

Bridger smiled down at her. "Not you Cavanaugh women," he said. "You're the strongest woman I know."

Laci wrapped her arms around Bridger, pressing her cheek against his solid chest. She cried for Alyson, for Tiff. For any others who had suffered because of Emma's pain.

Bridger held her, smoothing her hair as the water beat down on them. Laci wondered if anything could wash away the stench of gasoline on her skin. Or the memory of Spencer and Emma engulfed in flames.

It would take time. The house was gone, completely destroyed. The flames had taken not just the house, but any memories of a life her mother and father had had there before her father was killed, her mother abandoning the house and her daughters.

Laci knew her grandfather Titus would take it the hardest. He must have thought that as long as the house stood waiting there was hope that his daughter Geneva would return to it.

Laci held out no such hope. She feared that whoever had sent the notes knew the truth: her mother had never left Whitehorse. Just as the photo album with Laci's and Laney's snapshots hadn't left. Would she ever know the truth? She doubted it. Some mysteries were never solved.

Gramma Pearl always said there was a little good hidden in the bad, something to ease the pain. Laci leaned into Bridger and let him ease the pain.

Chapter Fourteen

Laci looked up as a gust of wind and the sharp, sweet scent of pine filled the front door of the restaurant.

Bridger burst in with the biggest Christmas tree she'd ever seen. "Thank the lucky stars that the ceilings in this apartment are ten-footers," he said, laughing. "I saw this tree and knew it was The One."

She couldn't help but smile as he stood the huge tree. It was magnificent.

"I know what you're thinking," Bridger was saying. "How will we ever be able to decorate such a large tree, right?"

"It did cross my mind."

He grinned, and she heard voices coming through the kitchen. She gave Bridger a questioning look as he leaned toward her and gave her a quick kiss.

Her heart leaped and her eyes blurred with tears as she heard her sister's laugh just before Laney burst through the kitchen door into the restaurant, holding an armful of Christmas decorations. Behind her was Nick, her husband and Whitehorse's newest deputy, with more decorations. They'd changed their plans and come home for Christmas, inviting all his relatives to Montana for the holidays instead.

Their grandfather Titus came in pushing Gramma Pearl in a wheelchair. Pearl cradled a bottle of champagne in her lap and gave Laci a half smile, eyes twinkling.

Behind them were the Bailey girls—Eve, McKenna and Faith—and Sheriff Carter Jackson and his older brother Cade.

Laci was surprised to see Cade. She knew he usually spent the holidays out at his cabin near Sleeping Buffalo. Christmas had been hard on him since his wife was killed in a car accident on Christmas Eve six years ago.

They were all laughing and brushing snow

from their coats as they put down the Christmas tree decorations they'd brought.

Laci hugged each and every one of them, kneeling down to take the champagne from her grandmother and plant a kiss on her cool, dry cheek. She was doing so much better, and Laci saw in her eyes happiness at being here.

"I have Christmas cookies!" Laci announced. She'd almost forgotten that she'd made the cookies before the grand opening of the restaurant.

While the men put up the tree, Laney came into the kitchen with Laci.

"How are you?" her sister asked, giving her a hug.

"I'm okay," Laci said. "I'm sick about the house, though. Is Gramps all right?"

Laney smiled and nodded. "I think he's relieved. He was talking on the way here about giving us each a piece of the ranch so we can build our own houses. Not too close but close enough our kids can play together."

"Our kids?" Laci laughed, then saw her sister's expression. "Oh, Laney, you're pregnant?"

Her sister nodded through her tears. "I just found out. Did I mention that twins run in Nick's family?"

Laci hugged her. "I'm going to be an aunt."

"So tell me about Bridger," Laney said.

And she did.

"You're in love with him," her sister said when she'd finished.

Laci nodded.

"And how does he feel about you?"

"Well…" How did he feel about her? "He gave me half of the restaurant as an early Christmas present."

Laney must have heard the disappointment in her voice. "Eve told me why he was here in Whitehorse. I asked Gramps about the sewing circle. I couldn't tell if he knew what Gramma had been up to or not. But he definitely doesn't know any details. I'm sorry."

"It's all right. I just wonder if Bridger will ever be happy until he finds out the truth about his birth," Laci said.

They took the cookies and glasses for the champagne out front and watched as the group finished decorating the tree.

"I saved the best part for you," Bridger said and handed her a beautiful glittering angel. He swept her up, lifting her so she could put the angel on top of the tree.

"Someone get the lights," Titus called. The room went dark.

Bridger's gaze locked with Laci's as he plugged in the tree. An array of colored lights flashed on, the tree glittering with ornaments. It was met with a chorus of oohs and aahs.

"It's beautiful," Laci sighed as she smiled at Bridger. "Thank you." She knew she was thanking him for more than the tree. He'd brought everyone together here today knowing how much she needed her family and friends.

"There's more," he said softly as he stepped to her. In the glow of the lights from the tree, he reached into his pocket and came out with a small jewelry box.

"The second part of your Christmas present," he said. "I can't wait until Christmas."

Her eyes widened in surprise as he opened the box to reveal a breathtaking diamond engagement ring.

She began to cry as he knelt down on one knee and said, "Laci Cavanaugh, I want you to be more than my partner in this restaurant. I want you to be my partner in life. Will you marry me?"

She couldn't breathe. For maybe the first time in her life she was speechless. She looked around the room at the faces of the people she loved. Christmas music played on the radio in the kitchen, and on Main Street she heard sleigh bells and children laughing.

She couldn't have envisioned a happier scene as she looked into Bridger's dark eyes and felt as if everything that had happened had been leading to this moment. Hadn't she always believed in destiny? Well, she did now.

"Yes," she finally managed to say, her voice cracking. "Oh, yes."

And then she was in his arms. Everyone was cheering and laughing. Her grandfather popped the champagne and someone turned up the radio.

"Silent Night" was playing. They stood, champagne glasses raised, Bridger's arm around Laci, and all sang as the lights on the Christmas tree glowed as warm as her heart.

"Merry Christmas," Bridger whispered.

"Merry Christmas."

Epilogue

As Christmas Day approached, it continued to snow. Huge white flakes drifted lazily down from the heavens. The Christmas lights came on in the park. Everywhere there were people on the main street, shopping, and carols playing on the radio.

A new year was approaching. It would be a time of joy and sorrow.

Pearl Cavanaugh was doing much better, but while she attempted to speak, the words were unintelligible. But given her determination, Laci and Laney had no doubt that their grandmother would recover her speech.

Eve and Bridger held out hope that eventually they would know about their births and might even find their birth mother.

Carter was still waiting for an ID on the

male body found at the old Cherry house. In the meantime, he'd set up a sting operation to find out who was selling drugs down in Old Town Whitehorse.

A kind of peace hung over Whitehorse as the snow fell and shoppers scurried along the street with brightly lit windows. A sense of hope that the future held promise, that all the bad times were behind the community.

At the state mental hospital, a patient on the criminally insane ward blinked and focused on the nurse's face in front of her.

"Doctor!" the nurse called.

"Where am I?" the female patient cried, looking around wildly, fear apparent in eyes that had been blank and unseeing for months.

"Easy," the doctor said, coming into the room and to her bedside. "Do you know your name?"

She nodded slowly. "Violet Evans."

The doctor smiled. "That's a place to start, Miss Evans."

"But what am I doing here?" Violet asked tearfully. "Have I been injured? Was I sick?"

"Let's just take it easy, all right. You've

been sick. I'll tell you everything. All in good time."

Violet nodded and leaned back. He was right about one thing: it was just a matter of time. A matter of time before she got out of here.

Wouldn't everyone in Whitehorse and Old Town be surprised to see her back? she thought as she smiled weakly up at the doctor.

"Tell me I'm going to be all right," she whispered.

"I think you're going to be just fine, Violet Evans. You have the rest of your life ahead of you."

Unlike some of the residents of White-horse, she thought with a smile.

* * * * *

Look for the next installment in the WHITEHORSE, MONTANA, series next month in CLASSIFIED CHRISTMAS *by B.J. Daniels*

SPECIAL EDITION®

LIFE, LOVE AND FAMILY

These contemporary romances will strike a chord with you as heroines juggle life and relationships on their way to true love.

New York Times *bestselling author Linda Lael Miller brings you a BRAND-NEW contemporary story featuring her fan-favorite McKettrick family.*

Meg McKettrick is surprised to be reunited with her high school flame, Brad O'Ballivan. After enjoying a career as a country-and-western singer, Brad aches for a home and family…and seeing Meg again makes him realize he still loves her. But their pride manages to interfere with love…until an unexpected matchmaker gets involved.

Turn the page for a sneak preview of THE McKETTRICK WAY by Linda Lael Miller On sale November 20, wherever books are sold.

Brad shoved the truck into gear and drove to the bottom of the hill, where the road forked. Turn left, and he'd be home in five minutes. Turn right, and he was headed for Indian Rock.

He had no damn business going to Indian Rock.

He had nothing to say to Meg McKettrick, and if he never set eyes on the woman again, it would be two weeks too soon.

He turned right.

He couldn't have said why.

He just drove straight to the Dixie Dog Drive-In.

Back in the day, he and Meg used to meet at the Dixie Dog, by tacit agreement, when either of them had been away. It had been some kind of universe thing, purely intuitive.

Passing familiar landmarks, Brad told himself he ought to turn around. The old days were gone. Things had ended badly between him and Meg anyhow, and she wasn't going to be at the Dixie Dog.

He kept driving.

He rounded a bend, and there was the Dixie Dog. Its big neon sign, a giant hot dog, was all lit up and going through its corny sequence—first it was covered in red squiggles of light, meant to suggest ketchup, and then yellow, for mustard.

Brad pulled into one of the slots next to a speaker, rolled down the truck window and ordered.

A girl roller-skated out with the order about five minutes later.

When she wheeled up to the driver's window, smiling, her eyes went wide with recognition, and she dropped the tray with a clatter.

Silently Brad swore. Damn if he hadn't forgotten he was a famous country singer.

The girl, a skinny thing wearing too much eye makeup, immediately started to cry. "I'm sorry!" she sobbed, squatting to gather up the mess.

"It's okay," Brad answered quietly, leaning to look down at her, catching a glimpse of her plastic name tag. "It's okay, Mandy. No harm done."

"I'll get you another dog and a shake right away, Mr. O'Ballivan!"

"Mandy?"

She stared up at him pitifully, sniffling. Thanks to the copious tears, most of the goop on her eyes had slid south. "Yes?"

"When you go back inside, could you not mention seeing me?"

"But you're Brad O'Ballivan!"

"Yeah," he answered, suppressing a sigh. "I know."

She rolled a little closer. "You wouldn't happen to have a picture you could auto-graph for me, would you?"

"Not with me," Brad answered.

"You could sign this napkin, though," Mandy said. "It's only got a little chocolate on the corner."

Brad took the paper napkin and her order pen, and scrawled his name. Handed both items back through the window.

She turned and whizzed back toward the side entrance to the Dixie Dog.

Brad waited, marveling that he hadn't considered incidents like this one before he'd decided to come back home. In retrospect, it seemed shortsighted, to say the least, but the truth was, he'd expected to be—Brad O'Ballivan.

Presently Mandy skated back out again, and this time she managed to hold on to the tray.

"I didn't tell a soul!" she whispered. "But Heather and Darlene *both* asked me why my mascara was all smeared." Efficiently she hooked the tray onto the bottom edge of the window.

Brad extended payment, but Mandy shook her head.

"The boss said it's on the house, since I dumped your first order on the ground."

He smiled. "Okay, then. Thanks."

Mandy retreated, and Brad was just reaching for the food when a bright red Blazer whipped into the space beside his. The driver's door sprang open, crashing into the metal speaker, and somebody got out in a hurry.

Something quickened inside Brad.

And in the next moment Meg McKettrick was standing practically on his running board, her blue eyes blazing.

Brad grinned. "I guess you're not over me after all," he said.

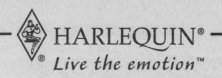

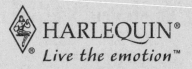

HARLEQUIN®

SuperRomance®

...there's more to the story!

Superromance.
A *big* satisfying read about unforgettable characters. Each month we offer *six* very different stories that range from family drama to adventure and mystery, from highly emotional stories to romantic comedies—and much more! Stories about people you'll believe in and care about. Stories too compelling to put down....

Our authors are among today's *best* romance writers. You'll find familiar names and talented newcomers. Many of them are award winners— and you'll see why!

If you want the biggest and best in romance fiction, you'll get it from Superromance!

Exciting, Emotional, Unexpected...

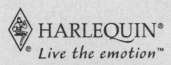

HARLEQUIN®
Live the emotion™

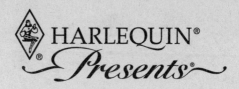
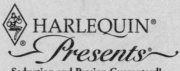

Harlequin® Historical
Historical Romantic Adventure!

Imagine a time of chivalrous knights and unconventional ladies, roguish rakes and impetuous heiresses, rugged cowboys and spirited frontierswomen— these rich and vivid tales will capture your imagination!

Harlequin Historical . . . they're too good to miss!

HHDIR06

SPECIAL EDITION™

Emotional, compelling stories that capture the intensity of living, loving and creating a family in today's world.

Modern, passionate reads that are powerful and provocative.

nocturne

Dramatic and sensual tales of paranormal romance.

Romances that are sparked by danger and fueled by passion.